# 3X KRAZY

# Lock Down Publications & Ca$h Presents

# 3X KRAZY
## A Novel by *De'Kari*

# Lock Down Publications
P.O. Box 944
Stockbridge, Ga 30281

Visit our website at www.lockdownpublications.com

Copyright 2020 by De'Kari
3X Krazy

First Edition November2020
Printed in the United States of America

*This is a work of fiction. Names, characters, places, and incidents either are products of the author's imagination or are used fictitiously. Any similarity to actual events or locales or persons, living or dead, is entirely coincidental.*

Cover design and layout by: **Dynasty's Cover Me**
Book interior design by: **Shawn Walker**
Edited by: **Kiera Northington**

## Stay Connected with Us!

Text **LOCKDOWN** to 22828 to stay up-to-date with new releases, sneak peaks, contests and more…
Thank You!

# Submission Guideline

Submit the first three chapters of your completed manuscript to ldpsubmissions@gmail.com, subject line: Your book's title. The manuscript must be in a .doc file and sent as an attachment. Document should be in Times New Roman, double spaced and in size 12 font. Also, provide your synopsis and full contact information. If sending multiple submissions, they must each be in a separate email.

Have a story but no way to send it electronically? You can still submit to LDP/Ca$h Presents. Send in the first three chapters, written or typed, of your completed manuscript to:

LDP: Submissions Dept
P.O. Box 944
Stockbridge, Ga 30281

*DO NOT send original manuscript. Must be a duplicate. *

Provide your synopsis and a cover letter containing your full contact information.

Thanks for considering LDP and Ca$h Presents.

## Thanks...

I would like to thank my team, my supporters and readers for keeping me focused. With my first book, I decided to shoot for the moon. Now here we are, seven books later and we are on track to reaching that goal. Seven down and ninety-three to go!

Destination: The Top
Current Position: Climbing

# Acknowledgements...

The goes out to all the Movements in the Bay: 3rd World, East Bay Dragons, A-Team, Gas Team, Stubby Ent., Nutt Case, AFNF, Babe Case, Soul Strippas, Broad Day, Steady Mobbin, Smack Mobb, Taliban, Neva Die Dragon's, Village Mobb, One Mobb, 101 Mobb, City Boys, 34 The Top to the Low, Bay View, The Point, Vietnam Valley, Lake View, Filmore, Potrero Hill, Alameny, Army Street, West Point Double Rock, Harbor Row, Lake View, Randolph St., My Choppa City Niggaz, Turk & Taylor, Sunnydale, Geneva Towers and Bayview. San Fran-Mothafuck'n-Cisco stand up! The Mannor, Young Nigga Nation, YG, MMN, Flat Line Boyz and Money Team. I love the Bay Area, "Cali" living.

Some of my supporters and readers have been calling me The King of Cali, much love and respect for that. I think it takes a lot to be a King. Am I a King right now? I don't know, but I'm going to shoot for it. I know that much.

Shout out to the Lockdown Family! This LDP Movement is crazy! TJ Edwards, you're killing 'em.

# Dedication

This book is dedicated to US. There's no I. Just WE for always, forever and eternity. All we got is US. As long as we got US, the rest don't matter.

One Aim, One Struggle, One Good!

Neva Die

# CHAPTER 1

## 1999

*I'm politicking wit dis chicken wondering if I should holla/ little brown skin chick from The Rich named Tasha/ coming through like I do, you know getting my bark on/ knew she was a thug cause when I met her, she had a scarf on/ 54-11 size 7 in girls/ Babyface that looked like she was an angel with curls/...*

That was me, a ten-year-old skinny, nappy headed, little rug-rat getting my mack on with my little cutie Tasha. DMX's new joint, *It's Dark and Hell is Hot* was banging out of damn near every radio stereo, and sound system in the hood. "How's It Going Down" was one of the hottest singles on the album. Here I was spitting every bar, word for word to Tasha as if it was my song and I'd written it for her.

Tasha was sitting on the stairs smiling from ear to ear, looking like an angel. While I stood in front of her performing my own little music video, courtesy of my older brother's Sony boom box. Which if he knew I was messing with it, he would fa'sho kick my ass. Ty'Reese, my older brother, was locked up right now facing murder charges over a dispute involving a female.

Police sirens could be heard over the music. From the sound of the sirens, they were pretty close, but I paid them no mind. Shit, this was Acorn Projects, West Oakland California's own baby Iraq. Acorn, as we referred to as the projects was one of the most active, crime ridden spots in West Oakland and its natives were very proud about that. Hearing police sirens or seeing police chases were as common as seeing a stray cat walking by or watching a piece of garbage fly by with the wind. Besides, I was tryna put on a

performance good enough to make Tasha wanna reward a nigga with a kiss.

The police sirens were getting so loud, they began drowning out the music. I was reaching for the volume to turn it up when Tasha suddenly called out, "Ooh! Jeffrey, look!" The excitement in her voice snatched my attention away from the radio. I turned around just in time to see the Big Homie Onions, sprinting full speed towards us with what had to be six or seven police cars after him.

Onions was a member of the A-Team, aka them niggaz you didn't want to fuck with. The A-Team had West Oakland on lock and was running the game. Onions was one bad mothafucka. I wanted to be just like him when I got older.

I quickly picked the radio up and moved out of the way, so he had a direct path into the building. I knew he would run into the building and ditch the police out of one of the many exits. This was an all-day, everyday occurrence. Next, I opened up the door leading inside the building. I don't know what made me do it. But like I said, Onions was a lieutenant for the A-Team and one of the Big Homies in the Acorns. Not to mention, one of my idols. My heart was beating rapidly in my chest while I held the door.

He never slowed down as he looked my way and smiled. He raced past us so fast as he shot through the open door that I almost didn't see the smile. That was one of the only times I'd ever seen Onions smile. As soon as he was through the door, I released my hold on it, letting it close behind him. Not before I noticed him toss something into the corner once he was inside the building. It was a good thing the cops hadn't gotten out of their cars yet, because they didn't see him toss the package.

The cops stormed into the building after him, some shouting orders and a bunch of codes I couldn't understand.

All of them had their weapons drawn. The look on Tasha's face told me she was scared.

"Fucking little nigger bitches!" one of the cops called out as he passed Tasha and me.

I guess he didn't miss what I had done for the Big Homie with the door. Fuck him!

He would get over it. I don't know why he was angry though. By the age of six, I had learned it was us against them. The hood against the police. If a six-year-old little boy was smart enough to know that, what was wrong with him?

Seconds later, it was just Tasha and me, outside the building by ourselves again. The only signs of what we'd just witnessed were the parked squad cars that sat with their lights still flashing. Tasha looked at me with a scared look on her face.

"Wait right here for a second," I told Tasha.

"What? Why, Jeffrey? What are you about to do?" I knew it was only her fear that made her fire off the questions. I could see it in her face. I just didn't have the time to explain to her what I was about to do.

"Just wait right here." There was no time to explain. "I'll be right back," was the best I could do for her.

I hurriedly crept inside the building before she could protest. My eyes went to the corner I saw Onions toss the package in. It was right there, waiting to be picked up. When you're raised in the hood, you learn early on it's survival of the fittest in the streets. Dog eat dog, etcetera, etcetera. Which means when you see an opportunity, you don't hesitate. You take it, which is exactly what I did.

Before any of the police could double back, or one of the nosy ass neighbors stuck their head out of one of the doors, I snatched the package up. It was much bigger than I thought.

Nervously, I shoved it inside my pants and walked back outside.

Tasha was standing up, looking at the door when I stepped back out.

"What's that?" she asked, immediately noticing the large bulge in my pants.

"I'm happy to see you," I joked as I reached down and grabbed my jacket off the stairs. I didn't know what was inside the package in my pants. But I did know that if Onions didn't want to get caught with it, neither did I. "Come on," I told Tasha after zipping my jacket up and grabbing my brother's radio.

I knew we had to disappear before more police showed up and decided to ask us some questions or worse, like the racist cop that came back and wanted to kick my ass for opening the door for Onions.

I walked Tasha back to her apartment. The entire way she wanted to know what was in my pants. Finally, I told her the truth. I didn't know what was in the package, but I was sure it was valuable. And I hoped it would change my life.

After that, we both openly wondered what the Big Homie had done this time. With Onions, you never could tell. One day, he was beating the brakes off of somebody. The next, he was shooting them. On his bad side was somewhere a nigga didn't want to find himself. Believe me!

After I dropped Tasha off, promising her I would let her know what was inside the package, I made my way to my homeboy Jay's apartment. I'd barely taken three steps before the sound of gunshots erupted through the night. I paused momentarily, silently praying the Big Homie was alright. Then I put some pep in my step and made my way to Jay's door.

It didn't take long, since he lived on the same floor as Tasha. Just on the opposite end of the hallway. Damn near all the lights in the hallway were either screwed out or knocked out. So, the hallway was dark. The darkness or night never bothered me though. I've always felt as if I was one with the night.

Miss Johnson, Jay's mom, answered the door after I told her it was me. The smell of her jasmine-scented incense was a heavenly welcome, after a person just walked through the old wine and piss-smelling hallway.

"Hey, Jeffrey! How are you doing, honey?" she asked, giving me that warm, friendly smile she was known for.

Miss Johnson was the exception to the rule when it came to parents in the projects. She worked for VTA, driving city busses instead of being on welfare. She didn't drink or use drugs. Most Sundays, you could find her in church instead of hanging out. It made you wonder what had happened to my best friend Jay. All I can say about Jay was he was the total opposite of his mother. But we'll get into that later.

"Hey, Miss Johnson, I'm okay. Is Jay home?" I asked as she let me inside.

"Yes, he's back there in his room. You can go on back there with your little handsome self. Do me a favor, honey, and tell that son of mine to make sure y'all keep it down. Tyrone's back there too and you know how the three of you get when you all get around each other."

*Ty and I have been friends since elementary. Yet, Jay and I have known each other for only a few years and it's crazy, because I am closer to Jay. Jay and I shared a brotherly bond, but the three of us were Three The Hard Way.*

"No problem, Miss J," I called over my shoulder as I was already making my way down the hall to Jay's room.

"I'm just saying though, it's three the hard way up in dis piece!" I called out as I opened the room door.

"My main man, Jeff To Da Left," Jay called out when he heard my voice. He didn't take his eyes off of the screen.

He and Tyrone were playing the new John Madden on his Super Sega.

"What's up, Jeff?" Tyrone called out.

People used to call me Jay as well, but it got kind of weird once Jay and I started hanging out. He was two years older than me, so naturally, I had to change my name.

Since I was left-handed, Jay started calling me Jeff To Da Left, which slowly became my new nickname. I closed the door behind me and told them to pause their game, I had something important to tell them. They paused the game after they finished the play on the football game. While they finished up, I was busy staring at his life-size poster of Aliyah. She was truly one in a million, like the name of her song.

"What's up, Jeff?" Jay broke my deep stare and brief fantasy about me and "Miss One In A Million." She was an angel taken away from us way too soon. I thought, *why didn't God keep her around long enough for me to make her my wife?*

I plopped down on the bean bag he had in the corner. "Nigga, yo mama told me to tell you we gotta keep it down." I looked at Tyrone, who was by for the loudest of us three "So… Ty, nigga, that means you gotta shut the fuck up."

"Nigga, I know you didn't have this nigga pause this game in the middle of this Oakland Raider ass whooping I'm giving him to tell us that bullshit," Tyrone snapped at me.

"Shit, nigga, my mom's rules ain't bullshit. You know she will come in here and Jesus Christ yo ass to death!" We all started laughing. She was a sweetheart, but Miss Johnson didn't have a problem preaching a nigga to death.

When I gathered my composure, I told them what happened with the Big Homie Onion while Tasha and I were hanging out by the back stairs.

"Man, that nigga Onions stay G'd up," Jay stated as he interrupted my story.

"You always cup-caking with Tasha, knowing you ain't even hit that yet. Fuck you think, you Ginuwine or somebody?" Ty was not only the loudmouth out of our little clique, but he was also the shit talker. I wasn't the type of dude to front, so my dudes knew I was still a virgin, but I wasn't stunting it.

"You don't need to be worrying about what me and my woman are doing. Nigga, you need to tell yo girl to save yo skinny ass some food, instead of eating it all up," I joked. Ty was messing around with this girl that was big as a house. He would always joke that big girls have good pussy. The two of them had been messing around for about two years now. Ty was a couple of months younger than Jay. They both had already lost their virginity and constantly let me know how much fun I was missing. Teasing me for being the only virgin in the group.

Ty started to say something, but I cut him off. I leaned forward in the bean bag and got all conspiratorial. "Look. What I didn't tell y'all was that as he was running, the Big Homie tossed a package. The police didn't see it and after they ran by, I snatched it up." My voice was down low, because I didn't want Miss Johnson to hear me.

"Nigga, what was in it?" You already know that was loudmouth Ty.

Jay just sat there patiently waiting.

I leaned forward so I could sit up straight. For some reason as I began unzipping my jacket, I took in the scent of Jay's

room, "Blue Nile." This was his favorite Muslim oil scent. The smell was bomb!

When I finally managed to pull the package out of my pants, which I had to stand up to do, Ty was the first to speak as usual.

"Nigga, hopefully it's money! We gonna be rich!" Neither Jay nor I commented.

The package itself resembled one of those black bags a barber keeps his clippers and stuff in. If it was money, it would be a lot, but it would nowhere near be enough to make us rich. When I unzipped the package, my eyes bulged out of my head. Ty's mouth hung wide open. Jay simply smiled and began rubbing his hands together like an evil mad scientist.

When I could finally speak, I looked at the leader of our clique. "Jay, is this what I think it is?"

"The only thing better than money." Jay stood up and walked over to me. When he reached for the package, I let him grab it. "My main man, Jeff To Da Left, that nigga Onions tossed his bundle and you found it. You're damn right, it's what you think it is. A package full of rocks."

Miss Johnson wasn't the nosy sort of parent. She'd rather trust the knowledge of living right she instilled in Jay, instead of spying on him. Because of this, we almost never had to lock the room door. Jay felt this was one of those times where it was important enough to do so.

After locking the door, he came back over to the bed and dumped the contents of the package out onto the bed. I couldn't believe how many bags came out of the package. It seemed like they would never end. There were twenty-one individual bags in all. The three of us each picked up one of the baggies. While Jay and Ty flipped theirs over and over, admiring its contents, I opened mine and began counting.

Soon, the two of them followed suit. When I finished counting the rocks, which were all individually wrapped in some sort of plastic, I had counted one hundred in total. When they were done counting, both confirmed theirs held one hundred as well. I randomly selected another one of the bundles and began counting it as well. So did Ty and Jay. Six bundles and all of them had one hundred rocks in them.

Jay said it was safe to say each bundle had one hundred rocks inside of it. Forget being safe. I was being smart. So, I grabbed another bundle and started counting. It took us almost an hour to count all twenty-one bags. Every bag contained exactly one hundred rocks of crack cocaine. The package I found contained twenty-one hundred rocks.

My come-up created two questions for us. The first question, how much was each rock worth? The second and most important question was, what were we going to do next?

*** **3X** ***

# CHAPTER 2

The three of us went over all the possible options we could think of, in regard to what we would do with the drugs. What it all boiled down to was this. Ty just wanted to be able to know what it felt like to have some money in his dusty pocket. Jay didn't care about his mama's feelings or the church; he was ready to become the next Felix Mitchell, Oakland's first major drug kingpin in the seventies and eighties. I, on the other hand, wanted to make the best choice possible. I agreed with Ty, I was tired of being broke. It's hard when you constantly find yourself being teased and being broke in the projects, full of broke mothafuckas. But when your mom was the neighborhood "Pookie," you really didn't have too many options.

At the same time, I was far from a dummy. I might not have known how much each rock was worth. But I was smart enough to know, if Onions was willing to go through so much trouble not to get caught with the package, it had to be a lot. Shit, two thousand and one hundred of anything was a lot.

The only thing we were able to agree on was the fact that we would talk about it again the following day. It was getting late and both Ty and I had to get home. We decided to leave the crack with Jay. Ty wasn't reliable enough to hold something like that and my mama was the biggest crackhead in West Oakland. If she found the package in my room it would disappear like the lost city of Atlantis. Jay's was the safest place for it!

Ty and I both lived in the same building. We lived in the last building at the back of the projects, so we walked together. He didn't shut up the entire walk, which made me extremely nervous. The streets had ears and I didn't need them hearing about our hidden treasure. I silently wished Ty would shut up.

Besides, I was more interested in thinking about what our best move would be.

When we reached our building, I stopped before entering and pulled Ty a little off to the side so I could let him know the severity of keeping his mouth closed.

"Ty, listen to me. I know you're excited. We all are. But you have to remember this shit belongs to the Big Homie Onions. Now we both know that nigga will kill us if he finds out we took his shit." The look on his face told me I had his full attention.

"You can't tell nobody about this, Ty, or you're going to get us killed. I'm serious, Ty. Don't say shit to nobody." I sounded like a father lecturing his son. Or at least that's what I thought a father would say to his son. None of us knew our fathers, so we did a lot of imagining of the things a father would do or say.

"I I won't say nothing, Jeff. You ain't gotta worry."

Something about the level of fear in his voice told me that just maybe, he wouldn't blab about this.

Shit, I was so scared. The whole time we were talking, I kept turning my head and scanning shadows. Making sure no one was eavesdropping on us. Maybe this added to Ty's apparent fear.

"Make sure you don't. Cause if I find out you did and the Big Homie don't kill us, I'mma fuck you up!" I know I curse like a sailor, but anybody who'd been forced to endure the shit I've been through would talk just as bad as me or worse.

After feeling confident I put the fear of God into Ty, I walked dreadfully to my apartment. The moment I opened the front door, my nose was assaulted by so many foul smells, it was a miracle I didn't pass out.

Our apartment made the stale, pissy hallway smell fresh. I did my best to try to clean, but a nigga couldn't do too much

with just water. Every time I stole some soap and cleaning supplies, my mom would sell them, so I said, "Fuck it!"

Now I would only steal the shit I needed to survive. Her and this raggedy-ass apartment were on their own, just like I'd been on my own all my life.

My story wasn't anything special. In fact, it was the typical "Hood Tale."

Pops ran off shortly after a nigga was born. Moms did her best to raise me by herself. Until the pain of Pops leaving became so unbearable, she turned to drugs, abandoning me like he abandoned her.

Yada, yada, etcetera.

Fuck 'em! They didn't want me, and I don't need them.

I was halfway across the darkened living room when the spark of light startled me. Over on the broken-down filthy couch, my mom's sat butt-ass fuck'n naked in all her natural horror. The spark was from her cheap lighter as she sat smoking crack out of a glass stem. I mean fa'real, fa'real, this mothafucka was asshole butt-naked, sweating like a Hebrew slave. Smoking in the middle of the living room, like she lived by her mothafuck'n self or some shit.

The foul stench of sweaty sex was in the air. From where I was standing, it smelled like she hadn't showered in at least a month.

She'd done so many fucked-up, disrespectful things over the years, but this by far took the cake. How could a mother behave like this in front of a child? I just shook my head in disgust and started to walk away. I didn't need her to see the tear as it made its way down my face.

"Fuck you shaking yo lil bitch ass head at me for, faggot? Mothafucka, this is my house! And I'll do what the fuck I wanna do in my shit!" She sounded like an angry hyena as she roared at me.

"You could at least put some clothes on or do that inside of your room." I was more hurt than anything. I couldn't believe she had so little respect for me that she would allow me to see her like this. I couldn't believe I was the one feeling ashamed!

"Bitch! Don't you come up in here wit yo little nappy headed ass, thinking you can fuck'n tell me what the fuck I can and cannot do up in my own shit! I do what the fuck I wanna do in my shit! It's your mothafuck'n fault yo father left in the first place. I should've flushed yo little bitch ass down the fuck'n toilet!"

This was the type of shit I had to put up with every mothafuck'n day since she started getting high. Let her tell it, everything was my fault. It was my fault that nigga left. It was my fault she was a dope fiend. It was my fault we didn't have shit. I was just a little kid. How in the fuck was any of this shit my fuck'n fault?

Just then, I heard the toilet flush. A few moments later, some nigga that resembled a Great Dane walking upright came out of the bathroom.

"Bitch! What are you out here fussing about now?" It seemed the disrespect was imminent tonight. I say that because the anorexic, dusty-looking Greyhound nigga said this as he came strolling out of the bathroom asshole butt-naked himself.

If the producers had wanted a black man to play Freddie Krueger, in the old *Nightmare on Elm Street* movies, this nigga would've been perfect!

When he saw me, he called out to my mom. "Sheila, who's this lil nappy head nigga?"

"Don't pay that lil bitch no neva mind. He ain't nothing but a fuck'n mistake." This came out of my mom's mouth, right before she relit her pipe and took a hit.

"Damn, lil nigga, I thought my mom's was a mean bitch."
He chuckled as he walked past me.

Filled with rage, hurt and humiliation, I stormed down the
hall to my bedroom. I would've slammed the room door, but
that would've only let her know she'd gotten to me and I
refused to give her the satisfaction. I used that same resolve to
hold back the tears begging to be released.

I hurriedly packed what I could into my old beat-up
backpack and headed back out of my room. I made it halfway
down the hall before I remembered something. I rushed back
into my room and grabbed Tasha's photo off my dresser. It
was a photo of her at her cousin Evon's birthday party. Tasha
had a mouth full of cake when the cameraman caught her
shoveling even more of the cake in her mouth. She looked so
happy and carefree in the photo. Just looking at it would make
me happy during the roughest moments.

I knew I would need the photo later that night. On impulse,
I snatched my brother's DMX CD out of the radio on my way
out. As I made my way down the hall, I silently wished I could
make it out of the apartment without her saying a word to me.
I'd learned a long time ago that prayers were never answered.
So, I stopped praying.

When I walked out into the living room, I got the shock of
my life. The skinny nigga was standing up in front of my
mother with his head tilted back. She sat her ass right there on
the couch with her mouth filled with his dick. I couldn't
believe that shit. I was more angered than disgusted. This was
clear proof that she had no respect for me, or herself whatever.
The sounds of the nigga moaning and whimpering like a lil
bitch wasn't nearly as sickening as the sounds coming from
her mouth.

Just then, the nigga'z head tilted down and he stared at me
with the slimiest smile on his ashy face. His yellow teeth and

eyes made him look even more suitable for the role in *Nightmare on Elm Street*. Just to egg me on and fuck with me even more, the nigga said, "Sss yeah, bitch, suck that big dick." To my horror, she began moving her head back and forth at an impossible speed. I was frozen, paralyzed by shock. The slurping sounds she was making were horrid. The entire ordeal only lasted a few seconds before I was able to break my paralysis. But it felt like forever.

It was at that exact moment Sheila, in my eyes, stopped being my mother. Or maybe I should say, she stopped being my mom, because she's never been a mother.

When I walked out, I didn't even bother closing the front door. Why should I? They didn't give a shit about me. Therefore, I didn't give a shit about them or their privacy. I was oblivious to everything. The pissy smell in the hallways, the night air, the sounds of Acorn's nightlife. None of it registered in my head as I walked through the projects. I was walking in a daze, my mind drifting in and out. I guess I was on autopilot, because I ended at Jay's home.

When she opened the door, I guess she could see it clearly written on my face.

"Aaww, you poor baby, come here." The moment I felt Miss Johnson's warm, secure embrace, my resolve melted. The dam busted and the tears flowed.

She pulled me into the living room and held me tight in her arms as I cried my soul out. Later, when I was able to talk, I told her what happened. I thought poor Miss Johnson would have a heart attack hearing about me witnessing my mama giving that nigga a blow job.

Miss Johnson's relationship with Jesus must have been good, because she just kept saying things like, "Oh, dear Jesus," and "Oooh, Lord Jesus, help this child!"

I didn't think telling her that her friend Jesus didn't answer prayers would've helped the situation any. So, I didn't say anything.

For a while, she kept starting like she wanted to say something, only to shake her head and catch herself. Finally, she just said a prayer. When she was done, she told me God would take care of everything. She told me that if I let go and let God, he would make sure everything was alright.

She got up to get some sheets and a blanket for me. While she was gone, I was mentally cursing that same white Jesus. He didn't give a shit about me. He witnessed firsthand all of the horrible shit afflicted on me. Because of that, I had no reason to believe in God and trust he would do anything to help me.

Miss Johnson walked back into the living room and made the sofa into a bed for me. She even kissed me on my forehead before walking out. Jay hated the love and affection his mom gave him. Yet, as she walked away, I found myself wishing I could've had a mother like Miss Johnson.

I pulled out my photo of Tasha. After kissing it, I sat it on the coffee table up against an incense bowl so I could still see her happy face.

The images of Sheila played over and over inside my head all night. Each and every time, I'd wish she was never my mother. All night I wished I had a moms like Miss Johnson. I wouldn't dare waste my time with prayer. Prayers didn't get answered. But I remember wondering if wishes ever came true.

*** **3X** ***

# CHAPTER 3

Something crashed against my head, waking me out of my sleep. At first, I was startled until my eyes adjusted, and I saw Jay standing over me, holding a pillow and smiling.

"Nigga, wake yo ass up! Over here invading my kingdom like our forces are weak or something." Jay had a look in his eyes like he was ready to set it off.

"Nigga, you better watch yo mouth before Miss Johnson hears you and comes out here and two-piece you," I joked as I sat up and rubbed the sleep out of my eyes.

"Moms got up early this morning. Apparently, there was some kind of disturbance late last night or early this morning. Old lady McDaniels called her and told her. Moms just came and woke me up and told me she'd be right back. It obviously was something important."

"How long did she say she would be gone?" I asked him as my own mischief gave birth to an idea.

"She didn't say. She just told me that under no circumstance were we to leave."

"Well, in that case. . ." I shot off the sofa before he had any time to react.

Jay was caught completely off guard as I tackled him like a defensive end for the San Francisco 49ers.

"Fumble!" I shouted when I hit him because the pillow he was holding went flying out of his hands.

We wrestled back and forth the moment we hit the ground. Jay and I were always tussling, wrestling and play-fighting. Just as lion cubs tousled and fought in the jungle, which prepared them for adulthood. Helping them hone-in their hunting and fighting skills. The streets were our jungle, and we were its lion cubs. Training for the skills we would need

29

to reign and rule over our kingdom. Even if we didn't know at the time, it was like our subconscious knew.

We wrestled and horsed around for a good ten minutes or so, before we heard Miss Johnson. "Uh-uh, that's enough, boys." When she spoke, we instantly stopped.

One look at Miss Johnson's face said it all. Something was seriously wrong. She had a look on her face like she just lost her best friend but was scared to admit it.

"Mama, what's wrong?" The alarm in Jay's voice was heavy. Instantly, his protective side surfaced.

"Javari, I need you to go in your room for a while. Mama has to talk to Jeffrey, baby."

I was scared I'd done something wrong. Yet, I didn't detect an ounce of anger in her voice. Suddenly, I became worried. Jay looked like he wanted to protest but I guess something told him not to. I could tell he was as worried as I was. However, he reluctantly did as Miss Johnson requested.

My little heart pounded away in my chest as my fear mixed with the anticipation of the unknown.

"Jeffrey, come sit with me on the sofa, honey." Her tone was tender and compassionate.

I stood up from the floor and slowly followed her over to the sofa. We sat in silence for a moment while, I guess, she thought over how to tell me whatever she needed to tell me. The wait reminded me of those times I knew I was going to get my ass beat but had to wait for the beating. My nerves were crawling all over my body.

Finally, she spoke. "Jeffrey, I know you've been through a tremendous amount of heartbreak and suffering in your young life. And I'm sorry, honey. The Lord works in mysterious ways. I won't sit here and pretend to know His ways. I only know that when our lives are destined for great things, we tend to suffer more—"

I couldn't wait any longer. I mustered up the courage to cut her off and ask, "Miss Johnson, what's wrong?"

She closed her eyes and took a deep breath just before saying, "Lord Jesus, please give me strength, Father."

When she looked at me, I knew I wasn't ready for whatever she was about to tell me.

"There was an accident early this morning. T-there was a fire, Jeffrey, at your mother's apartment. The fire department tried their hardest to put the blaze out, but I'm afraid they couldn't do it in time." I just sat there looking at her dumb founded.

"Jeffrey... I am sorry, honey, but your mother and her friend didn't make it out of the apartment in time." Tears were flowing from Miss Johnson's eyes.

I was stunned silent.

I stared straight at Miss Johnson, but I didn't see her.

All the fucked-up things Sheila had done to me popped into my mind.

Those were the images I was seeing in front of my eyes. Images of cruel torturous memories replayed like nightmares right in front of me.

"A-a-are they dead?" My voice sounded foreign to me. Like someone else had possession over my voice.

"I'm sorry, Jeffrey, yes. They both died in the fire." I didn't understand why Miss Johnson was crying, her and Sheila weren't friends.

In fact, Sheila talked bad about Miss Johnson just about every chance she got. Which was all the time.

I'd be lying if I said I could remember anything at all about the rest of the conversation. Miss Johnson continued to talk. No doubt she was probably trying to console me, but I didn't pay any attention to a single word. I allowed myself to be

distracted by all the memories that hounded my consciousness.

I hadn't realized I was crying until Miss Johnson dapped my wet eyes with some tissue. She then handed me the tissue. I wondered if she'd think I was the Devil if she found out I wasn't crying because I was sad. I was crying because of the memories and also because I was finally free from all the abuse and heartache.

Instead of saying anything, I stood up and walked to Jay's room. Silently!

From the look on my nigga'z face when I walked in, I could tell he had heard everything. I didn't care, Jay was like a brother and I didn't keep anything from him anyways. Unless it was about Tasha.

"Damn J, I'm sorry, man." His level of sincerity was understandable, but Jay's words threw me for a loop.

"Sorry for what?" What the hell did he have to be sorry for? He didn't do shit.

"What else? Sorry about yo moms."

"Shit man, Miss Johnson's been more of a mom than Sheila ever was! Don't be sorry for me." I wasn't trying to give Jay shit for trying to be a friend. I just didn't know how to tell him that I didn't feel any loss.

"Yo Jeff, it's me, man. You ain't gotta play tough with me. You just found out you lost yo moms, so it's okay to be upset." I could hear irritation coming from his voice.

"I'm just saying though. It ain't about being hard, brah. You can't miss something you ain't never had. Sheila ain't neva been a mom to me. I ain't lost shit!" I hope Miss Johnson didn't hear me because I'd raised my voice a little that time.

As I was talking, I walked over and sat on the bed next to my best friend. Jay reached over and placed his hand on my back.

"Don't stress, Jeff, you still got me. You'll always be my little brother. Straight up!"

"You all I got, Jay," I stated.

"Naw brah, we all we got!"

It's crazy but my nigga had more love for me than my own so-called moms.

*** **3X** ***

### Six days later

The days came and went, but to me they seemed like one long, tedious day.

I was in the room with Jay and I heard Miss Johnson arguing with someone. I had never heard Miss Johnson raise her voice. When things went quiet and I heard the door close, I walked out the room and asked her what was wrong. She told me Children Protective Services (CPS) was trying to take me away and lock me up in some kind of home for boys. Imagine that! Here it is, I haven't done anything wrong, but the first thing they want to do is lock me up.

Miss Johnson wasn't having none of that. She promised me she wouldn't let them, and I believed her. I didn't say anything to Miss Johnson, but I was in total agreement with her. I wasn't about to let those white folks lock me up.

On top of that, today was Sheila's funeral and Miss Johnson was making a big fuss over it. Which I couldn't understand, but it was something to help me take my mind off of the CPS people.

The weather was a mirror image of my life, dark and filled with gloom. The sky looked like a storm was coming. Perfect omen for what was building in me emotionally. I sat silently in the backseat next to Jay on the way to the church. The

services were being held at Miss Johnson's church, Allen Temple Baptist Church. As I rode in the car, I stared out of the window looking at nothing, wondering what catastrophic event was next to fuck things up in my life.

Without warning, the car began getting pummeled by dime-size pieces of hail. Maybe God wasn't done beating my ass. Miss Johnson was always telling us nothing could happen without God allowing it to happen. I must've pissed Him off at some point in my life for Him to allow so much fucked-up shit to happen to me. By the time we made it to the church, the hail had turned into bone-chilling sleet.

"Come on, boys, we're going to have to make a dash for the door if we don't want to get drenched," Miss Johnson told us as she pulled into the parking lot of the church.

We both muttered some form of agreement. I didn't give two fucks about the suit I was wearing. I just didn't want to be rude to Miss Johnson. She was always so kind to me.

Miss Johnson thanked God for blessing us with finding a parking space close to the door. It's funny how church folks are always thanking God and giving him credit when good things happen, and they are so quick to blame the Devil for the bad shit. If you ask me, that ain't cool. Why didn't they ever give the Devil a chance? What if he didn't do half the shit people accused him of? I know it may sound crazy to some people, but this was the thought going through my head. To be so young and see evil in my own mother. I didn't believe the Devil made her do it, she was just plain evil

Before getting out of the car, I saw Tasha's mom's truck a couple of spaces over from where we parked. The Escalade with the candy-grape paint job and 28-inch rims was the only one in Oakland that looked like it. Everybody knew that truck belonged to Miss Carla, Tasha's mom.

Once Miss Johnson parked the car and turned off the motor, we simultaneously opened the doors and made a quick dash for the opened doors of the church. Halfway to the church I heard Miss Johnson's alarm being activated. *Beep! Beep!*

She must've pushed the button while we were running. Either the sleet wasn't as bad as it seemed or Miss Johnson's God really had her back, because when we got inside the church, we barely had anything on our clothes.

We made our way down the hall into the main lobby that led to where everybody was waiting. When we walked through the doors, I was surprised to see so many people. I would later find out Miss Johnson had asked her pastor to preside over the funeral, as well as requested it to be held at her church. Most of the people at the funeral were members of the church's congregation. Here and there, I spotted a familiar face amongst a sea of strangers.

We followed Miss Johnson up the aisle to the front of the church. The air inside the church was stuffy and I could barely breathe. The sweat that ran down the back of my neck gave an uncomfortable fit to the dress shirt, which made the suit jacket feel like it was suffocating me. To make things worse, it felt like everyone in the room was staring at us. Still, I refused to hang my head low in grief. Instead, I walked with my head held high with a blank expression on my face.

Both Miss Johnson and Jay sat with me on the front row. If they had sat somewhere else, I would've been sitting all by myself. After I'd sat down, I heard someone softly whisper my name. When I turned around to see who called me, my eyes landed on Tasha's beautiful hazel eyes. They were filled with sadness. She smiled a sort of sad smile and whispered, "I'm sorry," just loud enough for me to hear.

I mouthed back, "Thanks." She smiled again and I turned around.

The choir sang a couple of old sad church songs before the pastor began talking. I don't have a clue what he preached about or how long he preached.

My mind was once again playing the same rerun it's been playing all week. Vivid memories of my fucked-up life on repeat. Jay nudged me in my side, bringing me back to reality. Music was coming from the organ. A line of people was in front of the casket.

For the first time, I noticed the casket. It was a soft lavender color with silver trim. I couldn't believe Sheila's lifeless body was laid up inside of it. Something as pretty as the casket was, held someone so hideous and cruel as her. Considering that this was my first funeral, I had no idea what to expect when I looked inside the casket.

A few days ago, I told Miss Johnson I'd never been to a funeral. She sat me down and went over the process. That is how I knew my time was coming to view the body. I slowly stood up. Somehow, my hand was inside of Miss Johnson's. It felt soft yet reassuring. I allowed myself to be led around the huge church until I finally came to a stop directly in front of the casket. I was two feet away from it, so I couldn't see inside.

Strangely, my heart was racing inside of my chest. It was hard to breath. Suddenly, it was very hot.

"I'm going to give you a moment of privacy, honey," Miss Johnson whispered in my ear before letting go of my sweaty little hand. She rubbed my back and stepped back.

I didn't want to take the last two steps and look inside the casket, but I had to. I needed closure.

My feet moved on their own. Suddenly I was there, looking inside the casket. Sheila's face didn't look real. It looked like a mask of some sort.

36

The firefighters were able to put the fire out before the bodies got burned. So, they were able to have an open casket. It was the poisonous smoke that killed Sheila.

She still looked hideous. Her ugly body was a deep contrast to the beautiful satin pillows inside the casket.

Everyone inside the church was quiet, except for a sniffle here or there. I took a deep breath and let it out real slow.

*"Well, here we are. The moment of truth!" I thought.*

"That poor baby," I heard some old woman call out.

I was ready! I hawked up the biggest loogie I could muster up. The effort caused me to make a lot of noise. "Eechtwoot!" I spit the slimy loogie directly into her black ass face. The slimy, gooey, snot filled saliva landed on one of her eyes and her nose.

"Oh my God!" someone called out.

"Did you see what he just did?" another asked.

"Lord Jesus!"

There were a bunch of other shocking comments and gasps coming from people all throughout the church.

Fuck Sheila and fuck all the people who were so concerned about what the fuck I just did. No one was concerned for me.

"Bye, you black bitch!" I said loudly. "Eeechtwoot!" I spit another loogie on her ugly face. This one landing on her forehead. Then I turned around and walked out of the church with my head still held high, with a satisfied smile on my face.

People looked at me in shock like I was the Devil himself.

All of a sudden, I became very weak. I collapsed on the front porch of the church. I was emotionally drained. My entire body was depleted. I just sat there staring aimlessly. The sleet had turned to a torrential rain. As the rain fell, the gusty winds blew. All of a sudden, the tears began falling from my

eyes. I was crying so hard, I never heard anyone come outside the church after me.

"Sssh… Hush now, honey, it's going to be alright." Miss Johnson sat down next to me and took me into her arms. She held me in her arms for the longest on the steps, as I cried my heart out.

*** 3X ***

# CHAPTER 4

I was in Jay's room, thinking about Sheila. I'm not even about to sit here and front like a nigga wasn't affected by Sheila's death. I just didn't understand why I cared one way or the other. I mean, on the one hand, she was my mother and I had love for her, no matter what. I still remembered the good years before the drugs entered the picture and ruined her life, our lives! Unfortunately, those happy times did nothing to erase the abundance of turmoil that followed Sheila's drug usage. The days of pain, embarrassment, abuse and the nights of hell. So, on the other hand, I was glad she was gone.

Jay wasn't around much. He'd already begun his dreams of becoming the next Felix Mitchell. Ty took the package that Onions had tossed and started selling the drugs at his grandmother's house. It was easy to sell the drugs at his grandmother's house, because she never left the back room, except to use the bathroom. His uncle Big Roc always sold drugs out of the house whenever he was home from prison.

I was also thinking about Onions. I learned he'd gotten locked up that night I was performing DMX's song for Tasha and he was running from the police. I guess the police were tired of people getting away from the projects. They didn't stop until they caught him. At least with Onions being locked up, nobody would come bother us about the dope we found.

"Jeffrey, come on now and eat, baby, dinner's ready." Mama J. called out from the front room. "Aww baby, Mama knows you're still upset, but you have to put something in your stomach. Even if it's just a tiny bit. Please!"

How could I say no to that? I turned around and went to go wash my hands. Then came back and had a seat at the table. The food on the plate in front of me looked better than it

smelled. Once she made her plate, she sat down and said grace.

"Dear Lord, our Heavenly Father, we thank you for the many blessings you have bestowed upon us. Father, we ask that you bless this food so it may be nourishing to our minds, body and soul. Lord, I send a special prayer begging you to look after my child, for it seems he's been led astray, Lord. Be it as we may, we just can't change fate. Please Father, keep my baby safe. We pray all of these things in your precious, wonderful son Jesus' name, Amen."

"Amen!" I repeated.

It broke my heart to know that Mama J. knew what Jay was doing and couldn't do anything about it. I often heard her in her room late at night, crying and praying for Jay. I wondered whose will was stronger, since she always said, "Let thy will be done." Was this God character's will stronger than Jay's will to be Oakland's top gangsta?

I cut a piece of the roast and took a bite just to appease her. The moment I did, an explosion of goodness went off in my mouth. The food tasted so good I instantly became aware that I hadn't eaten anything in days. Seeing me eat, Mama J. kept smiling and saying, "Thank you, Jesus." She would say things like, "All the sheep are just as important to the good shepherd."

We were halfway done with dinner when Jay walked in. He walked right up to Mama J. and kissed her on the lips. The show of affection embarrassed me.

"Go on in there and wash your hands while I fix you a plate." Mama J. wasn't going to yell at him. That's not how she was. But while Jay was washing his hands, Mama J. was busy saying a prayer of thanks to God. I guess His will was stronger than Jay's. At least it was that night.

After dinner, Jay and I went to his room to play video games. John Madden Football was a favorite pastime of all niggaz in the hood, young and old.

"Jeff, when you gonna get out of your funk and come play the trap with me?" Jay asked me while we were playing the game.

"I don't know, Jay, I'm really just not feeling shit right now."

"Nigga, you feeling this Madden."

"That's about all I'm feeling too." I thought about it for a minute and decided to take a risk and say what I felt. "Jay, Blood, I'm not even gonna lie. While you out there trapping, Mama J. be in here going through all kinds of headaches and worry." Trapping is what we call selling drugs and hustling.

"Man, let me find you here falling in love with my mom and shit. Worried about her feelings and all," he joked as he intercepted the football from me in the game.

"I'm just saying. I've been here witnessing her going through it. I mean, literally losing her mind, behind you being out there in them streets. I know you, Ty and me, talked about what we were going to do and all, but I don't think I'm cut out for that street shit. I think I'mma give this God character a shot, cause nothing else seems to be working." I wish I could share my guilt and remorse with my brother, but I really hold true to being super, stitch lipped.

"Jeff To Da Left a Bible-toter, naaw I can't see that. Come on over to the trap and get some of this money." To add emphasis, he pulled a few wads of cash out of his pockets. "You already know I got your cut right here," he said, shoving one of the piles over to me. It looked to me to be at least ten thousand dollars.

"Now, all that's yours, like usual. But come on, Jeff, just imagine how much more we could make if you were there

with Ty and me." Jay had been trying to convince me all week to join them.

"I don't know about Bible-toting, but in the morning, I do plan on telling Mama J. I'm going to church with her." I paused and turned towards Jay so he could see how serious I was. "If this God nigga turns out to be some sort of hoax or some bullshit, then I'm with you full-fledge, no questions asked. All gas, no brakes! Right now though, Jay, I gotta do me."

He stared at me for a long time, looking like he was thinking over what I had just said. Sounds of gospel music could be heard coming from Mama J.'s room.

Finally, Jay spoke. "Jeff, you're my BFA, my brotha from another mother. Blood, I'll hold you down and support you, no matter what you do. If you wanna go holla at God, Moses, Jesus and some other niggaz, it's good. I got you. I'mma keep getting your cut from the package and when you decide to turn to the streets, I'mma be ready for you."

"Thanks, Blood." We embraced in a single-arm brotherly hug.

Afterwards, we went back to playing Madden. All the while, I thought about God, everything that had happened and what I wanted out of life. I didn't know if God was going to be the answer, but I just knew deep down inside the streets wasn't it for me. I wasn't built for the streets. I was made for something much greater than the streets, but only time would tell!

*** 3X ***

# CHAPTER 5

## (2009)

"Jeffrey! Baby, please make sure you are extra careful with that platter now, honey. We know Mother Daniels will have a personal fit if something was to happen to that Gooey, Gooey, Coffee Cake. " I knew Mama J. was going to call out to me before she did it. I smiled to myself at the thought.

The two of us have grown so close these past ten years that most people believed Mama J. was my biological mother. To me, she was. I've been calling her Mama J. now for about the last three or *maybe four years. I've been doing it out of love and respect, but mostly love!*

"Come on, Mama J., now you know that I am not about to allow anything to happen to this cake. Not even Armageddon itself could harm this cake." She laughed at this.

Mama J.'s cooking was legendary in Oakland, California. But now her baking skills have been made world famous ever since she appeared in *O Magazine*. And yes, I am talking about Oprah Winfrey's, *O Magazine*.

In my mind, I've already made reservations for at least three VIP seats in my stomach for slices of this cake.

Today was Easter Sunday. The church was having its annual Easter Sunday Easter egg hunt for the children. Afterwards was the big monthly "pot-luck."

Since living with Mama J., I've grown to like church a great deal. I didn't quite grasp or understand all of these concepts about God and spirituality. But I believe there was a Hell because I've lived in it. Which meant there had to be a Heaven and I wanted to see it. I believe from the Hell I went through with Sheila, I deserved to go to Heaven or at least see it.

Speaking of Sheila. Two things happened that day after her funeral. The effects of death reared its ugly head to a young Jay and me, causing the two things. I began to ask Mama J. more questions about this God she was always telling us about. Jay, on the other hand, realized life was too short and could be gone at any moment.

He decided that night he was determined to run the streets as soon as possible. He wanted to be a street king and wasn't going to allow death to come and stop him before he'd done that:

*"Jeff To Da Left, you up?" I heard Jay call out to me from his bed.*

*Of course, I was awake. I was too confused not to be woken up. Maybe it was that confusion that began my curiosity with God in the first place. Here I was, laying on the floor, crying in the pillow that Jay gave me to sleep on. Crying cause I was sad Sheila was gone.*

*How could I be sad though, when at the same time, I was glad she was dead? I was torn between the happiness I felt when I learned my abuse was finally over, and the sadness of losing a mother that I never had in the first place. This turmoil left me angry because I couldn't understand it. Mama J. told me it was called grieving. She said everyone dealt with grief differently. I didn't understand what grief was until she explained it.*

*"Yeah, I'm up, Jay. I can't sleep," I responded. I was up because I was feeling guilty about what I had done.*

*"Me either, Blood." He paused for a moment, then asked me, "Jeff, why do you think people die?"*

*After a while, I told him the only thing that made sense to me. "Because everything dies."*

*"Yeah, I know.... but why is that?" he persisted.*

*"Don't know."*

*"Do you think anybody knows?"*

*"Um, I don't know, maybe Miss Johnson."*

*"Maybe... naaw, my mom don't know." I rolled over so I could face his bed.*

*"Well then, maybe... Oh I know, maybe that guy God she's always talking about. Remember she said He knows everything?" I felt I'd just solved the problem.*

*"So where was he then?"*

*"Maybe if we go back to church with Miss Johnson, we will find him."*

*Jay didn't say anything after that for a long time. The only way I could tell he was still awake is because of the way his breathing sounded.*

*"You know what, Jeff? That God nigga sounds like a fake ass nigga to me. I'd rather get it how I live, like the A-Team, than to listen to some bullshit God talk. In fact, Fuck God! He ain't rock'n with us. So, I'm not rock'n with Him!" he finally said.*

*I didn't know what to say to that. So, I asked him. "Who are you rock'n with then?" I shouldn't have asked him that!*

*"I'm rock'n with the A-Team!"*

Thinking back on that night, I can say Jay made true to his word. He had a run-in with M.A., Onions, Zoe and some other niggaz from the A-Team. He stood his ground and earned their respect. Then it became official, Jay was A-Team, and I lost my best friend. Mama J. is the one who truly lost, because she lost a son. Jay has been in and out of juvenile hall ever since. I grew closer to Mama J. and church. I did this to fill the void in my heart and the loss of my friend.

I thought Jay would've been here at the church celebration today. I was really looking forward to it. He had been in juvenile hall a whole year this time. He used to talk about giving God a chance and coming to church. Mama J. and I

went to visit Jay every week the entire year. We even had Bible studies on Sunday with him. I think during that year, Mama J. was the happiest I've ever seen her. Which only made her heartbreak that much more severe, when Jay came home two days ago on Friday, telling us that he changed his mind about God and giving church a try.

I was so distracted thinking about Jay that I didn't see Reverend Jacobs as he was coming out of his personal chambers.

"Whoa there, young Jeffrey!" His calling out to me and my extremely quick reflexes are the only reason I avoided disaster.

"I'm sorry, Reverend Jacobs, I must've zoned out there for a second," was the excuse I gave for my not being focused.

My racing heart joined the sweat on my brow as the two culprits to betray how sorry I would've been, had I bumped into him and ruined the cake. The shakiness of my voice was a big help as well.

"It's okay. Let us just thank the Lord that an accident was avoided. Yes indeed! Thank you, Jesus!" The reverend was always super excited or turned all the way up as we like to say.

I made my way to the kitchen fully focused. Mother Daniels was already in the kitchen, making a massive pot of gravy to go along with her famous deep-fried turkey. The main ingredient to the gravy was turkey gizzards and turkey necks.

Most people didn't know the secret to her special flavor, but I did. She fried the turkey necks and gizzards in a big pan with bacon and pork chop grease, before making the gravy out of it. Mother Daniels revealed her secret to me.

"Now the good Lord told me that my dear ole Alice Johnson knew this here little old lady was praying for some of her miracle coffee cake. Unh-huh, yes he did." I didn't know

46

how she knew it was me that came in the kitchen, because her back was turned when I entered. But she didn't give me much time to think about it.

"And yes, Lord, that child even had the good sense to send it with my favorite little angel! Now Jeffrey, come on over here and set that on the counter and give Mother Daniels some sugar."

Astonished with her psychic ability, I did as she told me. All the while, I was thinking that all of the sugar in the world was in their food. The two of these women gave us all kisses of joy every time we ate their food.

"Where's that other little one at now? Our sweet little prodigal son who has lost his way. I heard a tale that he was perhaps going to bless our presence with his glorious appearance this morning." She looked so hopeful as she inquired about Jay.

"No, Mother Daniels, I'm sorry but he didn't make it this morning. I think he's sick."

"Now Jeffrey, you listen to Mother Daniels, you hear me? Don't you be in God's house telling no bald-face lie, even if your intentions are good. God doesn't like that."

"I'm sorry, Mother Daniels."

"Now it's okay, baby. Sometimes the Devil gets a grip on us that's so strong, only God Himself could shake loose. Now if it's the Lord's will, that baby will come back around. Now you just wait and see," Mother Daniels assured me after the hug and a kiss on the cheek.

It was a couple weeks until my sixteenth birthday. I don't know why but kisses from the Church Mothers were beginning to make me feel uncomfortable. That morning was no different. As I left the kitchen, I felt weird, almost like when a young boy's mother kissed his cheek in front of the school in the second grade.

I headed back outside to help Mama J. finish unloading the food from the truck. It was a beautiful morning, which was a good sign that it was going to be a beautiful day. Just not as beautiful as Tasha was standing in the doorway in her Easter Sunday dress.

"I hope it doesn't take you long to unload Mama J.'s truck. I would like it if we could have some time before service starts to hang out," she told me as I came walking up, carrying a large pan of jalapeno cornbread.

"It won't take long at all. This is the last thing." Tasha and I would just hang out and talk every chance we got. Sometimes we didn't even hang out, we just talked.

Before I had a chance to hear her response, Mama came walking up behind me.

"Good morning, Tasha. Now girl, don't stand there and be the reason this son of mine drops all of that delicious cornbread. Girl, you know he gets clumsy every time he gets around you." The two of them had a good laugh.

"I don't get clumsy, Mama. Things just get in my way all the time." This caused them to laugh some more.

Their laughter made me smile. These two, by far, were the most important women in my life.

I made it to the kitchen and back with a little extra pep in my step. Tasha was looking amazing. She was leaning her back up against Mama J.'s Expedition, reading her Bible when I walked back out the building.

She was wearing a light blue or powder blue floral dress. The flowers were a bouquet of colors. It also had white silk fringes along the edges. Long white socks came just below her knees. It was what one would expect a young lady of seventeen to wear to church. She just made it look breathtaking.

"Why are you looking at me like that?" Tasha asked me when she looked up from her Bible.

"I'm just amazed at how beautiful you are." At least I didn't sound as goofy as I knew I was looking.

"Jeffrey, why do you tell me that every day?" She blushed.

"Because every time I see you, I'm amazed all over again." Majority of our face-to-face conversations began this way. I loved it.

"I saw your brother yesterday. I'm glad he is home, but Javari hasn't changed, Jeffrey. I'm not a snitch, so I won't put his business out in the streets. So, don't even think to ask me what I saw. But I'll tell you this. I shouldn't have seen what I saw." Tasha wasn't gossiping. She loved Jay just as much as I did. She was just tired of seeing Mama J. get hurt, which was happening so frequently now it was becoming normal.

"He's only been home one day and already he's my brother instead of our brother?" I asked with a small attitude.

"Don't start that, Jeffrey, because you know how much I love that big-headed little boy. My brother's name is Javari Johnson, not J. Roc. I told you, I don't know J. Roc, who is exactly who I saw him being yesterday." She sounded hurt, not angry.

Just then the church bell began to ring, bringing our conversation to a pause, because it was never ending when it came to my brother. We discussed him a lot. Never argued over him or behind him, but we talked constantly about him.

Like normal, Tasha and I sat next to each other during the morning service. Allen Temple Baptist Church is one of the largest churches in Oakland. With such a large congregation, no one ever paid any attention to the many notes Tasha and I repeatedly passed one another.

She and I had been going together now for seven years. It was like we were one brain that operated two completely

separate bodies. That was how close she and I were and everyone who knew me, knew I was head over heels for her.

After morning service, the children had their Easter Egg hunt. I help the ladies get ready for the potluck in any way I could. Although I did this out of the kindness of my heart, they always rewarded me with a plate big enough for two.

Things were beginning to wind down by the time Tasha and I sat down to eat our meals. It was mid-day, and the weather had a Caribbean feel to it, that just put people in a good mood.

"Tash, we've been girlfriend and boyfriend for a minute now. Seven years to be exact, well... seven years, four months and six days." She was looking so beautiful as she blushed when I broke the time down.

I continued with my speech before I lost my nerve. "If we were grown, I would marry you and build you your own castle. Since we're not, I silently but impatiently wait for the years to roll by so that I am able to fulfill that dream. I'm not going to lie to you though. You get more beautiful as each day passes on to the next and I'm afraid of losing you—" This is when she interrupted me.

"Jeffrey, you don't have to worry. I'm not going anywhere. You don't have to worry about no other boy—" It was my turn to interrupt her.

"Tash, I'm not worried about no boys. Soon you are going to attract the attention of grown men, because you are so beautiful. Your beauty, plus the way that your body is beginning to develop, is going to drive these guys crazy and that's what I am afraid of." I let her hand go, which I had been holding across the picnic-style table we were seated at and reached into the pocket of my slacks.

I stood up and walked around the table until I was at her side. Never taking my eyes off of hers.

Once I was standing in front of her, I reached for her hand again.

"I know I'm young in age, Tash, but not in heart nor mind." I got down on one knee. "When I was a child, I did childish things. Now as a man, I put childish things aside and do as a man." I don't know who said the Bible didn't have "game," because I was quoting it and it was "game" that I was spitting!

"Tasha Renee Robinson, I know that you alone are the woman I want to marry, start a family with, and enjoy life with. Since I know what I want, I'm not going to play games with mine. I want you to be my wife." She looked like she was going to pass out from sheer shock.

"We can get engaged now and married later. Tash, if you're sure like I'm sure and love me like I love you, please will you be my wife?" *Whew*! *I did it*! I thought.

Now it was all up to her. A nice calm breeze blew by, preventing the perspiration that wanted to form on my forehead from doing so.

Just when I began to get nervous, she spoke.

"Jeffrey, whether it's today, right here right now, or ten years from now. I vow, you have nothing to worry about. Only you can ruin us. Yes, I will marry you. You little, big-head boy!"

*Clap*! *Clap*! *Clap*!

I thought someone was coming to steal my thunder. Rob me of my joy! I turned towards the sound of the clapping and couldn't believe my eyes. But my smile increased.

"Now that's what the fuck I'm talking about," he somehow managed to mumble around a drumstick sticking out of his mouth. Taking it out, he told us, "I'm glad that a nigga didn't interrupt this moment."

Jay was standing on the other side of the table, staring at us, smiling from ear to ear. At this moment I could not have been happier.

I jumped up off my knees, bringing Tasha with me. With us both standing, I gave her a big hug and kiss. Then I ran around the table jumping up and down saying, "Thank you, Jesus," over and over and gave my brother a bear hug.

"Did I happen to witness what I think I did?" I let go of my brother and turned towards the sound of Mama J.'s voice.

I instantly forgot about Jay and rushed into Mama J.'s arms, whooping and hollering.

"My wife! Mama! My wife! She told me she would be my wife!" I was so excited I was shouting.

All three of them were laughing at my silliness, but I didn't care. When I thought I couldn't have gotten any happier than my brother being there with me to witness my miracle, my mother ended up witnessing it as well. Things were perfect!

# CHAPTER 6

In the weeks that followed Easter, Tasha and I were inseparable. If we weren't outside together somewhere, we were on the phone. Our conversations went all over the place, but it didn't matter. I just wanted to hear her voice. The sound was heavenly.

On the morning of my birthday, she'd awakened me at exactly midnight, and we talked all morning, well past the sun coming up. After Tasha and I finally hung up. I got fresh to death in an *Iceberg* outfit and some retro Michael Jordan's. Mama J. brought me a necklace with a Jesus head on it, so I was bling blinging. It was my sixteenth birthday, and you couldn't tell me anything.

Mama J. threw me a birthday party / BBQ at Lowell Park, a few blocks from the projects and it was jumping. Everybody and their mama showed up. People I knew as well as people I'd never seen before. But they were from the hood, so it was good like that.

By 2:00 p.m. the only person that hadn't shown up was Jay. Before leaving the apartment that morning he told me that he had a few things to take care of out in the streets. He gave me his word that he wouldn't allow anything to cause him to miss my BBQ. So, when he hadn't shown up by 3:00 p.m., I knew something was wrong. From that moment on, I stopped enjoying my day. I was too sidetracked and worried about my brother and I could tell Mama J. was too.

Reverend Jacobs and the church had bought me the biggest and best present I received, a brand-new, 2006 Dodge Charger. After discussing it over with Mama, Tasha and I jumped in my Charger and went to go look for my brother. At first, Mama didn't want me to leave. I promised her all I would

do was roll down some streets in the hood and see if I could see him. After all, he wasn't answering his cell phone either.

Tasha and I drove all around the West, while listening to gospel music. She was uncharacteristically quiet, as was I. I think we both felt in our hearts something was wrong. I personally was saying prayer after prayer to my savior to be with and protect my brother.

From the Acorn's, we headed down Adeline towards The Alphabets, which was another hood near ours. I went through every hood in West Oakland. Even though some of the hoods were beefing with others, no one knew my car, so I was good.

We hit The Bottoms, Dog Town, Ghost Town, Cypress Village. Hell, we even went through the Alphabets again. I was a hundred percent convinced by now that something was wrong.

When I called Mama and she told me no one had heard from him still. I pulled over and said a prayer out loud.

I was driving down Adeline, headed back to Acorn when I spotted his Dodge Challenger parked by the liquor store. I pulled over and immediately jumped out after throwing the gear into park. I was excited and happy I had found him, yet still slightly nervous. He usually didn't go as far as 34th Street, because of the beef the A-Team had before the feds ran an indictment against them two and a half years ago.

A bad feeling shot through my body when I walked up to the driver's side door and the window didn't roll down. Especially since the car was running.

By this time, the sun was beginning to go down, which made it that much more difficult for me to see through the tint on the window. I lowered my head to be able to get a better or closer look.

When I saw the silhouette in the driver's seat slumped over, my birthday became the worst day in my life.

Consequently, this would become the last time I celebrated my birthday.

Standing there on 34th and Adeline at the store, looking at my brother's dead body, I realized there would never be any reason for me to celebrate that day. I snatched the driver's door open only to confirm my suspicion. My brother was dead. His brains were splattered all over his cocaine-white interior. The inside of the car smelled like a mixture of copper and shit.

"Tash, call the police," was all I could get out before I dropped down to my knees and silently cried. My world was shaken. I knew the remaining members of the A-Team on the streets were beefing with somebody, but brah assured me that the beef was nothing. This didn't look like nothing to me!

I don't really recall hearing Tasha scream when she came to see what I discovered. Nor do I remember my nigga, Gusie-Bo coming across the street from his apartment to see if I was okay after hearing Tasha scream. I just know these things happened. The entire hood talked about it.

I never knew how much love my brother Jay had in the hood, until someone stole him from us. At his funeral a couple of weeks later, it felt like all of West Oakland showed up to pay their respects and say good-bye. I watched everybody that came, with paranoid-schizophrenic eyes. Any one of them could be the person who robbed my mother of her chance to see her son graduate high school. To see him have his first child.

Something dark overcame me. Something very dark, I can't really put a description to it. But on the day of Jay's funeral, something overcame me that would never allow me to remain church-going, God-fearing, happy-go-lucky Jeffrey. That day, I became Jeff To Da Left. I wouldn't fully embrace that revelation, but I felt it.

Later, it was just Mama J., Tasha, and Ty at the cemetery on top of 66th Avenue and MacArthur. The weather was cold, dark and gloomy. A perfect match with my mood.

Earlier that day at the church, they played Boyz II Men's "End of the Road" and I couldn't get the melody out of my mind. Over and over it played in my head, and tears rolled down my face.

No one seemed to know anything about what happened to Jay. The streets weren't talking at all, which was a very unusual thing. Usually when someone got killed in the West, everybody knew about it. However, when it came to my brother, nobody knew shit!

I wasn't buying it. Fuck that!

I knelt down on one knee and grabbed a handful of loose earth.

"Brah… damn, Brah. A nigga don't know why you left me. We were supposed to get older and take the world by storm. Batman and Robin, Ren and Stimpy, not no shit like this." I didn't mean to disrespect Mama J. with profanity. I was just numb. "Now this wasn't supposed to happen to us. Three the hard way, remember?"

"Three the hard way." Ty ghostly repeated off to the left behind me.

Suddenly, Mama J. erupted with a loud shrill of a cry. Her voice echoed away in the night. I ignored my pain momentarily and stood to give my mother a hug and to hold her.

We stayed in that position for only God knows how long, before I made the decision that it was time to leave. The four of us remorsefully and regretfully climbed into Tasha's Chrysler 300 and slowly pulled off.

*** **3X** ***

*Immortalized! Blood-shot red, my eyes / When the gunshots spread the skies, it ain't nowhere to hide / I swear to God a credit card can't account for the hate / Boy it's too late there's no escape, we already planning yo wake.*

Later on that night, Tasha and I were sitting inside my parked Charger in the back of the projects. The music was playing low as we were sharing a bottle of Hennessy one of the neighborhood dope fiends had gotten for us.

"Tash, babe tell me why God is allowing the Devil to treat a nigga so bad? No matter what I try to do, it seems like He pops up just to knock me down a few notches. When I turn to God for help, He doesn't come through. Where is He at, Tash? I thought He was always here?" I asked her after a long swallow.

I wasn't a heavy drinker, so I was feeling the bottle of Henny. That plus a nigga'z grief had my emotions all riled up and ready to get stupid.

"Shefferey, this ain't got nuttin to do with God," she slurred my name as she spoke. Obviously, the Hennessy was affecting her. "This is all the Devil's doing, not God's, Shefferey." Even though she slurred, I understand her loud and clear.

For a long time, I didn't speak. My mind drifted off to so many different places, I'd lost my train of thought twice. Even still, I was holding my liquor better than her.

"Tash, now I know every decision I make henceforth not only concerns me. I know that by you agreeing to marry me, your life is affected just as much by my actions as mine." Again, my mind trailed off.

This time it was her that brought me back to the present. "Shefferey, what are you tryna tell me?"

Just then I noticed how many degrees it had gotten hotter inside the car.

"I'm gonna find 'em, Tash."

"Find who? Shefferey?"

"Tash, I'm going to find the people that stole our brother from us. The people who killed Jay." I could feel my blood getting hotter than the temperature in the car.

"They murdered him, babe."

"And I'm going to murder them!"

# CHAPTER 7

## Two Days Later

I was driving down 8th Street, headed towards the Lower Bottoms. My only thoughts since Jay died were of revenge. God who? Brah I didn't know him anymore. I knew grief and Hennessy.

A few years back, Ty's people up and moved across Cypress into the Lower Bottoms from what Jay used to tell me. Ty was claiming the L.B. as well. Which was cool, because Ty was still our folks. In fact, Ty had started hustling a little while after Jay started. They were both getting money, while I was developing a relationship with God.

Since everyone on the streets was stitched-lipped over what had happened to my brother Jay, I decided I was going to take it to the streets. If nobody was going to talk, I was going to make somebody speak.

I was on my way over to see Ty to let him know about my decision to jump in the game.

"Jeff To Da Left!" Ty called out as I pulled up to his spot.

"What's good wit it?" I asked as I hopped out the whip, greeting the blazing sun.

"Aww, you know, dis 'Town Bizzness' shit," he responded with a big smile on his face. "What brings you from the church?" Ty asked.

"Fa'sho. You know I know what time it is." My attention drifted off to two niggaz were standing close by. A little too close for my comfort. And paying a little too much attention to Ty and me.

When he picked up on my vibe, Ty told me, "Aw, those are two of my little cousins. They moved over here from San Francisco a little while back, they cool!"

That relaxed my nerves a bit, but I still kept my eyes on them. I didn't know what it was, but something just didn't sit right with me in regard to the two of them.

"In that case, you know how we rock. Family of my family is without a doubt, family! And an enemy of my enemy, would be considered family as well." This was our mantra.

"Naw... this ain't nothing to do with the church. My nigga, I'm just not feeling how ain't nobody got nothing to say. Usually niggaz can't wait to run and tell some shit, but when it comes to our brother, ain't nobody know shit. I ain't feeling that."

"I mean, Jeff, you don't understand how it be out here in the trenches. It's hit and miss, dog eat dog, kill or be killed. If ain't nobody saying shit, it's because either ain't shit to say, or maybe the risk of saying shit is too high." What Ty was saying sounded like some bullshit.

"What the fuck is that supposed to mean?" I couldn't even remotely begin to understand that shit.

"When everybody got their ears to the streets tryna hear something, so does the person with the most to lose, like the killer. Now, what if the killer is someone you might not want to know that you're inquiring about his or her business? That alone will shut the streets up and shut niggaz the fuck down. You know, Town niggaz fully support the 'Stop Snitching Movement', shout out to AJ, Wayne Perry and them niggaz from Junior Black Mafia."

I couldn't believe the shit I was hearing. On the one hand, it sounded like a bunch of bullshit. Yet, on the other hand, everything he said was true.

"Nigga, I ain't scared of nan nigga in these streets! I'm going to find out who killed my brother and when I find out, I'm going to kill his ass!" I was beginning to get pissed off at Ty.

I was starting to get the vibe that he just didn't give a fuck. I could have been tripping, but to me, he wasn't as pissed off or hurt as he should have been or as much as I was.

*How could he not, though?* was the question in my head. This was our brother. Our A-1 from Day-1.

"Nigga, what the fuck yo ass know about these streets? Nigga, you can't hit yo knees out here in prayer and ask God to remove the Devil. Shit nigga, out here you got to remove the Devil all on your own." At that moment, he pulled a black gun off his waist and showed it to me.

"The only thing holy that the Devil respects and fears out here, are these holy mothafuck'n bullets in the .40." Although we were talking about the Devil and the streets, his gesture felt more like a warning to me.

"I don't give a rat's ass about what the Devil fears. To avenge my brother, I'm jumping two feet, ten toes deep into the game. As for the Devil, that bitch ass nigga should fear me. He remembers before this church shit, I didn't give a fuck, and I fa'sho don't give a fuck now! I owe this to my brother. He would've done the same for me!" I hadn't realized I'd raised my voice until somebody opened the front door of the trap spot!

"What the fuck is all that noise?" The nigga standing in the doorway resembled Deebo, actor Tom Lister, in the movie *Friday*. His body was completely covered with prison tattoos that made his enormous muscles look even bigger.

"Ain't shit, Unc. Just my brother letting off some steam about our brother getting killed the other day. He's taking it a little harder, that's all." Ty was talking to his uncle.

All of my life I've heard about the legend known around the city as Big Roc, Ty's uncle. His name put the fear of God

in niggaz all throughout Oakland. East, West and North. He just got home from prison.

He didn't put fear in me though. I fear no man, woman or child! Nothing walking this Earth.

"You little mothafuckas better keep that shit down! I need my mothafuck'n sleep tonight, cause I got a big job." Big Roc called out before slamming the front door shut.

"Ole grumpy ass nigga!" Ty spoke out loud before turning his attention back towards me. "Look Jeff, whatever you want to do, I'm with you one hundred percent. I'm just saying we got to be careful how we move. We don't need whoever it is we're after to know we're after them, before we know who the fuck it is we are after. Jay was my brother as well, brah and I'll ride for him, just like I'd ride for you," Ty swore.

"Say less then."

I spent the next ten minutes telling Ty what I had in mind. We decided we'd meet up later, so he could put me up on game as far as how shit was going down in the West, in regard to hustling.

*** 3X ***

After leaving Ty, I decided to swing by ¼ lb Burger. I was hungry as hell and had a taste for one of their famous burgers. I turned on to San Pablo Street, listening to some Kirk Franklin gospel music to soothe my mind.

When I pulled up, there was a nice size crowd already in the parking lot. I drew some attention because of the music, but it didn't faze me. Not everybody had to listen to some gangsta shit. For the most part, I ignored the stares I received, but I did return some.

People had the misinterpretation that because you were a child of God, you automatically had to be some sort of punk

or something. Maybe the old Jeffrey would have turned the other cheek, but Jeff To Da Left was Old Testament fire and brimstone.

While waiting in line, I saw this girl named Margo that went to school with me. She was a couple of people in line ahead of me, with her older brother, Byron. Once she noticed me, she made her way over to where I was standing.

"I see you don't care where you're at. When it comes to God you are all the way turnt up, huh?" That's how Margo began the conversation. We both got a laugh out of that.

Margo was a year or two older than me. She was about five foot four and built like a mega-stallion. I mean, even at seventeen years old, she had an ass that would give Kimmie J a run for her money.

"Why not? Everybody else is always repping what they like without a problem. Why can't I?"

"There's no law that says you couldn't," she agreed and followed by saying, "I'm sorry about your brother."

Instantly my mood changed.

"There's no reason to be sorry. You didn't do it. But thank you for your concern." Sorry wasn't going to bring my brother back to me. Neither was feeling sad and down.

"You know, Jeff, I'm not trying to be messy or anything. But you don't find it strange that usually when someone is killed, the streets be buzzing with all the latest gossip? But with Jay nobody knows nothing?" I didn't know if she was just being innocent or if she'd asked the question on some nosy shit.

It made me look at her brother in a different light. Could she have been asking because he had something to do with it? Was my brother dead because of her brother? My mind was beginning to go places that people didn't normally speak on.

"Why? What have you been hearing? Do you know something about Jay?" My demeanor changed instantly.

"W-what? No, I don't know anything. Why would I? I was just pointing out how everybody was acting all Secret Squirrel, G-14 classified." Margo's surprise was genuine. I could see that. Which made me feel fucked up for how I came at her.

By now, people in line were looking our way, being all nosy and shit. I was beginning to get pissed off. I wasn't the type of cat to lose my cool, so I took a slight deep breath, recalculated and then used the situation to my best advantage.

"Honestly, Go-Go." Go-Go was Margo's nickname. "I've been thinking along the same lines. It's like people know something but are scared to talk." I paused for a minute and watched the watchers, making sure they would hear me, because as far as I was concerned any and everybody was suspect.

"But I promise you, whoever did it, they fucked up! Jeff the church-boy is dead and gone. Jeff To Da Left is about to wake this bitch the fuck up! I promise you, from Doggtown to North Oakland, dese niggaz are about to feel something that they ain't never felt before. I promise you that." I looked each and every watcher in the eye and made sure everybody heard that shit.

"What the fuck he gone do, roll 'round the West playing gospel music all day?" some nigga who was standing behind Margo's brother said, under his breath. But I still heard that shit.

Mama J. always said, "There's no time like the present." I believed that as well, so I walked over to where the nigga was standing and got all up in his shit.

The nigga looked to be around his late teens or early twenties. He was just an inch taller than me but outweighed

me by about twenty pounds. Which is saying a lot, because I was checking in at five-nine and a hundred and ninety pounds.

"My nigga, you tryna get something off your mothafuck'n chest or something?" This was way out of my character to the people who've known me the last couple of years but to everybody else, it was a sign.

"What? Come on, homeboy, everybody can see you on some Bible-toting, Dear God please help me shit. So why you all up here, tryna pop some gangsta shit…."

*Bang*!

I'd heard all I needed to hear. I gave the nigga a right-handed haymaker. It didn't drop him, that wasn't my plan. I was about to put down a demo that was going to set the stage of my rebirth! He stumbled backwards. I was on him. Two jobs with the left overhand right cross followed by a left hook that did drop him.

"Dear God, in the name of your son, Jesus, I beg you to forgive this bitch ass nigga for asking for this ass whooping." I mocked my prayer loud so everybody could hear me and gave the nigga time to get up.

When he did, he put his face down and rushed me. His first mistake was getting in my business. His second one was underestimating me. His last mistake was that move!

I timed the uppercut perfectly. I stood him completely up. From the way his eyes swam in his head, I could tell he was punch drunk.

I fed him an eight-piece with a biscuit and knocked him out. If anybody knew Acorn, they knew we grew up fighting. We all had hands and had no problem facing a nigga toe-to-toe and making an example out of him.

By then, Go-Go's brother had their food and was ready to go. He called out, "Right on, Jeff To Da Left. They should have named your young ass, 'Watch the Left'." Everyone

started laughing. Over all of the laughter, he called out to me, "I know you a serious little dude so when you ready to do you, count me in."

That part shocked not only me, but I'm sure everyone in line. After all, Margo's brother already had a name for himself. For him to say he wanted to be down with me, was like a Mafia Capo giving you his blessings.

Margo and I said our goodbyes and then I stepped up to order my food. The loudmouth nigga was still out cold when I drove off.

*** **3X** ***

# CHAPTER 8

Tasha was waiting for me on our favorite stoop when I drove up. I grabbed the food and walked over to her.

"Hello, beautiful," I sang out, kneeling down to give her a kiss.

"Hey, babe," she responded, reaching into the bag and pulling out some fries.

I sat down next to my baby and pulled all of our food out. Once that was done, I got at my plate like it stole something from me. I wasn't worried about how I looked. I was hungrier than a refugee.

"What's this I'm hearing about you jumping in the game?" Tasha asked me, in between bites.

She didn't sound like she had an attitude, so I didn't take her question as a loaded question. Besides, she was way too direct of a person for me to think she would be sending subliminal messages to me.

"After our talk the other night, about Jay and getting revenge for his death, I've been entertaining the idea of doing that."

"But babe, why would you be thinking about that? What good is you going to the streets going to do, except for possibly putting you in a position where I might lose you as well." I could hear concern and worry in her voice.

"Tash, babe, you don't ever have to worry about something happening to me and I'mma tell you why. Most niggaz in the streets don't think. They let their pride and emotions navigate and steer the ship. Babe, you know me, I'mma think everything through twice before I move. That's just how I am. Plus, even though I may sin a little, God will continue to watch over me because I am his child. I am still

anointed." I wasn't running a game on my baby. This was how I really felt.

Tasha took another bite of her double bacon and swiss cheeseburger. I knew she was thinking over what I said, I could tell by the way she was softly humming to herself. She always did when she thought.

After a while, Tasha looked me straight in my eyes. Do you promise I won't lose you?" She was the one asking, but I was the one whose heart was racing.

"I can't promise not to worry you, because there is no way for me to know how you are going to respond to every situation." A look of worry came back over her face, so I quickly answered, "But I promise you, none of these niggaz in the game can faze me. They are not ready for me, babe. I will stay smart and move strategically." I know she was scanning my face for truth and sincerity. I was dripping with it.

"In that case, babe, find the niggaz that killed our brother and remind them that Revenge Is Promised." She looked at me with a look I've never seen in her eyes before. She leaned into my face real close as if she was going to kiss me and said, "I meant it, Jeff. Anybody who was involved, anybody who knew and didn't say shit, you better kill them."

That night, after talking to Tasha, I got on my knees and had a long conversation with God. I needed Him to understand my soul would not be able to rest without my brother being able to rest in peace. I also needed God's assurance that He would continue to love me unconditionally as the prodigal son I was about to become.

Before I lay my head to rest that night, I stood by my brother's bed after talking to God. I vowed to Jay no matter what it took, no matter where I had to go or what I had to do,

I would avenge his death and take care of his mother. Our mother!

An hour after I began talking to God and Jay, I climbed into my bed, which was right next to his bed. Jay and I had slept side by side in matching twin beds since the day I'd moved in, until the day he was taken. I cried myself to sleep thinking of my brother and all the fun we had.

In the middle of the night I was awakened by the soft sounds of someone crying. Initially, I was startled, thinking I was hallucinating. Then I realized the sounds were Mama J. She was laying on Jay's bed, crying into his pillow and talking to him. Laying there awake, I felt like I was eavesdropping on her. Like I was witnessing something I wasn't meant to witness.

Finally, that night, I decided to begin honoring the promise I made to Jay. I was going to be there for Mama J., so I climbed out of my bed and took the four steps it took to reach Jay's bed. Pulling back the covers, I climbed in bed behind Mama J. and held her. She was in the middle of talking to Jay as I did so.

"Please baby, please come back to Mommy. I need you, Jay... Dear God, why? I need my baby." She cried, heartbroken.

"It's okay now, Mama. I got you. Sssh, I'm here for you," I assured her, wrapping my arms around her from behind.

"Thank you, baby. Thank you. Jay, I knew you'd come back for Mama." She scooted her body backwards to me. I held her tighter. I guess in her distress she thought it was her son Jay holding her.

"Sssh, It's okay now, Mama. It's okay, I'm here." My heart became heavy as I held her in my arms. I wasn't going to do anything to add to her pain or to strengthen her sorrow.

As her body molded into my embrace, I could feel her sorrow. Her pain made its way from her body and slowly seeped into my heart and soul.

As I held Mama J. in my arms, Jeffrey Rasheed Watkins slowly died. A God-fearing, Bible reading, spirituality seeking, man slowly passed away.

Mentally, emotionally and physically, "Jeff To Da Left" was reborn and a monster was created.

*** 3X ***

"Jeff To Da Left, you gotta make sure you are ready for that shit. This ain't the church, where you can sin and then ask God to forgive you. The moment you bust that thang, it's over, 'Gonzo-Ponzo!' Ain't no asking for forgiveness going to bring these niggaz back once we send them on their way." (Gonzo-Ponzo means gone, ain't no coming back.) Ty was trying to school me like he was an O.G. or something.

Ty had received word about some niggaz on 34th and Adeline, over by where Jay was killed at, bumping their gums talking shit about Jay.

We were on our way to silence them niggaz.

Ty had been talking big shit ever since he'd picked me up that morning. He was driving, I was in the passenger seat, silent. The two little niggaz that was with him the other day were both sitting behind us. It turned out the two little niggaz were twins.

"Brah, fuck all that talking shit. Just get us to where these niggaz at and we'll see what's what!" I was tired of listening to Ty run his mouth.

I'd bet he'd never caught a body in the first place, I thought. Ty was always bumping his gums.

I reached over and pressed play on the CD player, 3X Krazy, a rap group out of Oakland was going crazy on the song.

*"The Dome Cracker, The Wig Splitta, The Grave Digga / all about my chedda, square ass nigga / Hate'n on a play cause I'm all about that fast cash / gunz go gitcha-gitcha when I hit chou block it's gone feel like a Gorilla/"*

Fa'sho I was feeling like a grave digga and a wig splitta!

As we pulled to the corner of 34th and Adeline, Ty spoke, "Those them niggaz right there in front of the store. Nigga, you still think you ready? Cause now is the moment of truth."

We were parked at the stop sign.

I looked across the street at the niggaz he was talking about. The Glock .40 became heavy in my lap. My eyes scanned the area. No cars were coming. There was no one else around.

I immediately picked up the .40 and opened the door. I barely let the door close as I made my way to the store in broad daylight. It couldn't have been later than noon.

"Man, I'm telling you, mothafuckas say'n the nigga Bamma upped that big thang, like you little bitch ass niggaz ain't ready for me..." one of the niggaz was telling the other.

"Is that what happened?" I asked. Neither one of them saw me until the moment I spoke up.

"Aw Jeffrey, what the fuck you gonna do with that?" the one that was talking asked when he noticed the .40.

*Bocca! Bocca! Bocca! Bocca!* "I don't talk to dumb niggaz."

The Glock answered his bitch ass and sprayed his thoughts all over the wall like graffiti. The nigga that was next to him froze like a deer staring at some headlights.

"Since you mothafuckas like talking and telling stories, make sure you tell everybody that Jeff To Da Left said Revenge Is Promised, nigga RIP."

*Bocca*! *Bocca*!

I needed the word to get out. Fuck the silence!

So, I left the second nigga on the ground squirming and crying like a bitch from the gunshots in his abdomen. I slowly turned around and made my way back to Ty and his two cousins.

Talkative Ty was quiet as fuck as I climbed back into the stolen car. He had a shocked look on his face which only confirmed my thoughts, that he ain't never killed shit.

"Instead of staring at me, now is the time when you drive off, nigga!" I brought him back to reality and turned the music up and listened to *3X Krazy*.

I looked into the Twinz' eyes through the rearview. There was no shock or fear in either of their eyes. They looked calm and bored. Which told me that they were B.T.A. (Bout That Action).

"Nigga, is you crazy or what? You just bounce out the whip and don't say shit! Broad daylight? And why did you leave the other nigga alive?" This was the first time Ty spoke.

"Ty as long as you've known me, you know I walk it how I talk it, nigga, and that's straight up. While yo ass was talking, I was walking. And as for the other nigga, he needs to bring a holy message."

"What the fuck is a holy message?" He looked at me like I'd lost my mothafuck'n mind. Deep down I knew I did.

"The Devil is coming and he's bringing Hell with him." I smiled to myself.

This was the first time I'd seen the Twinz react. They smiled too!

"Ty, I don't know what you got going on or what you've been into. But I'm telling you now, I'm about to take over West Oakland. You need to decide if you fucking with me. I can tell you right here and now, it's going to be a bumpy ride. But from what I see in your cousins' eyes, if we stick together, we'll always come out on top. The moment we don't, we won't." I'll let him think about that for a minute, because I knew I'd just dropped something hot on his plate.

"Say, Jeff To Da Left, we don't know how Big Cousin is feeling right about now, but Kane and I both 'feel' how you move. So, if you got plans on some big shit, we want in. Killing is what we love and we can already tell that fucking with you we gonna be very happy." Abel spoke for the first time since I met them! His twin Kane had still yet to speak.

This time it was Ty that spoke up. "Nigga, I don't even know why you're getting at me like shit sweet. You already know I'm riding 'til the wheels fall off. All gas, no brakes!"

We pulled up in front of their uncle's house.

"Then it is what it is. All gas no brakes," I repeated.

Then, for the first time Kane spoke up. "Fuck all that! Nigga, dis "Gas Nation." Fa'sho we all in and fa'sho we gone win!" He had one helluva sinister smile on his face as he spoke.

And like that, the Gas Nation was formed.

*** **3X** ***

# CHAPTER 9

I was turnt all the way up! All gas and no brakes!

A little while after that drill I just put down by the store, we received word about some other suckers that supposedly said something or knew something. I didn't give a fuck which it was. A monster was created when they stole my brother. No, I take that back. Fuck a monster, nigga, a mothafuck'n Devil was born!

I was riding with the Twinz, since Ty had some shit to tend to regarding the trap. It was all good with me though. The Twinz were on some next level murda shit from what I heard. I could tell that was real info I'd heard.

"Again, so the little chick says the front door is completely sealed off and boarded up. Which means only the back door can be used. So, we're all going in the back. Jeff, once we're through that door, you need to secure the front of the house, Big Homie. Kane and I will secure the rest." I decided to let Abel call the play since it was his drill. Plus, this would give me a chance to see the shit I heard about them, close-up and personal. I needed to know that I had some stone-cold killahs with me.

For the last hour, the only movement has been the neighbor smoking cigarettes. He's had three of them since we've been here.

"Yeah, I got you, lil brah. But let me ask you something. Since your brother doesn't talk, how are we going to know if he gets into trouble?" I thought that was the most logical question of the day.

"Don't worry, he won't get into any trouble." I wanted to push the issue, but the finality in which he spoke made me shut the fuck up!

The house was a single-story brownstone. We'd been watching it for an hour already and I was beginning to get antsy.

"I advise y'all to load up. We move as soon as the neighbor over there finishes his cigarette."

I didn't have to be told twice. I was already ready. Kane just merely smiled to himself. Three minutes later, we were rounding the corner on the side of the brownstone to the backyard. The night was pitch black, which helped conceal us as we crept across the backyard.

I reached the three-step porch that led up to the house. Just as I was getting ready to kick the door in, Abel held his hand up to stop me. He leaned forward and checked the doorknob. The door opened with no resistance. Silently, we poured in.

As planned, they went towards the back and I headed towards the front with my faithful gun in my left hand. On that first drill, that was my first time shooting someone. This Desert Eagle in my hand didn't jam on me, so to me, it was my trusted faithful gun.

As I neared the living room, I heard a TV on. I peeked my head around the corner and for sure, this nigga had his back to me watching a porno on TV. *Poor bastard couldn't even get no pussy*, I thought as I crept up behind him.

On the screen, some nigga was giving this thick redbone every bit of what had to be about thirteen inches in her ass. She was taking it like a champ. Talking big shit, trying to get him to fuck her harder.

O'boi on the couch was so caught up in what was going on on the screen, he never had a clue that I was there. I reached back and then cracked him across the back of his head at the exact moment I realized what was really going on.

"If you utter one sound, I swear to God, I'll send you to the Devil." It's a good thing she had a mouth full of dick. I

guess it gave her a chance to think about it, before deciding not to scream.

When I walked into the room, I thought he was jacking off while watching the porno movie. But when I walked up on him, I saw a cute little redbone on her knees, sucking his dick. God damn, she was thick!

"Stand up and put your clothes on, and then sit down right next to him," I instructed her, trying not to get sidetracked by her body.

A few moments later, Kane and Abel came walking in the room with a Ving Rhames looking nigga and a chick. I noticed Kane had some blood on him. When Abel saw me looking, he said, "Ole buff nigga was having a threesome. The other bitch tried to be a hero." That was all he said.

I shrugged it off!

"Porn star here, was balls deep in her tonsils. He never saw what hit him." I turned towards the other female. "I don't kill women and children. If you sit down and shut up, you'll live. But I promise you, if you utter a peep or give us a problem, I'll have my little one kill you too. Do you understand me?" I stared deep into her eyes to make sure she got what I said. She shook her head yes.

"Good, now sit down next to her."

I walked over by porn star, then stood in front of the nigga on the couch and slapped the living shit out of him to wake him up. He woke up startled, looking around like he was lost.

"M-man, who da fuck is y'all?" He tried to sound tough, but it wasn't working.

I slapped him across the head with my gun. "Bitch-ass nigga I'm the only one doing any talking up in here, unless you answering questions. You got that?"

"M-man, if you want the money, it's good. I'll give it to you."

This was one stupid mothafucka. I guess he didn't understand English. I slapped him again. The buff nigga looked like he wanted to do something bad to me. The nigga I slapped was crying and moaning. If he would've shut the fuck up, he wouldn't be in so much pain.

"Now, let's try this again. Cause my nigga, I don't give a fuck about yo money. Nigga, dis Gas Nation! We got money. We're not here for yo lil change. We're here to figure out which one of you two niggaz know something about who killed our brother Jay. Cause the word on the block is, one of you sure have been speaking on it."

The buff nigga spoke up. "Man, I don't know what or who the fuck you talking about. You killed my bitch over some shit I don't know nothing about." I swear to God he sounded like he wanted to cry.

"I didn't come here to play no games, nigga, is it you?" I asked the first nigga, ready to crack his shit again.

"W-what, N-n-no man, I don't know shit."

"Come on, brah, one of y'all know something."

They both kept repeating themselves.

I looked at Abel. "Do you believe them?"

In response, he just shrugged his shoulders.

*BOCCA! BOCCA! BOCCA! BOCCA! BOCCA!*

I shot both of them niggaz. I told them I didn't come to play games. I had to walk over and give the buff nigga a head shot just to make sure he was dead.

"If you want to live, go get your driver's licenses." Both the girls rushed to get their licenses out of their purses.

Once they both came back with the licenses, I looked at each one of them. "If the police find me, we will find you. Got it?"

They were so frightened they could barely move. I didn't know how the Twinz felt about leaving two witnesses, but like I said, I don't kill women or children. Period!

# CHAPTER 10

*"You don't want no drama… I sit on yo block rowdy / But you don't want the drama I bring / I bring beef to da White House… death to yo front door / You niggaz talk about it… Blow you ain't neva seen war / you ain't neva seen more goons than the Ghoulies / or a murda scene… shit you only seen in da movies / Niggaz wanna shoot me? What's wrong wit they murkin / I slide through they block and leave that whole bitch jerk'n /"*

I was bumping Dem Hoodstarz, featuring Young Felons, "Definition." My cousin across the waters put me up on them. I was listening to them on my way to pick Tasha up from West Oakland Public Library, off 19th Street and Adeline. Tasha had come across some books by Author De'Kari, called *Gorillaz in The Bay.*

After school, she'd catch a ride over to the library and read for a couple of hours. This was her new thing since Jay died. As I was pulling up to the front, I saw my baby in the center of a crowd, arguing with some nigga.

I stopped and threw the Charger in park. I bounced out right there and ran up to see what was going on. No one paid attention to me as I came up.

"Bitch, ain't nobody stupid. The whole West is talking about it. Niggaz is saying yo punk ass boyfriend did it…" the nigga she was arguing with was saying.

"Nigga, I just told you, I'm not about to be too many more of your bitches." Tasha was all up in the nigga'z face. She didn't see me coming.

That was just like my baby, she didn't allow anyone to disrespect her.

"Bitch, don't be—"

I heard all I needed to hear. "Say, you ole bitch ass nigga!" I called out, cutting him off and catching him off guard. "If you got something for me, what you sweating and pressing a woman for?" I was all up in his shit now.

The nigga instantly started shaking like a minibike. "S-say, Jay... I-I'm just saying. Mothafuckas saying you got something to do with my big brother's death."

Just like I thought, the nigga was all bitch, pushing up on a female. People began snickering and mumbling under their breath. Some were even laughing.

"Fuck that's 'pose to mean?" I smoothly pulled my Glock off my hip. I had tucked it as I was running across the street.

"Nigga..."

*Bam*!

The moment he opened his mouth, I busted him upside the head with the Glock. My first blow split his temple. Blood ran down the side of his face. Even still, I had an example to make. Right there in front of the library and the crowd, I pistol whipped the shit out of him.

"The next... mothafuck'n time... you fix you ratchet-ass mouth... to speak to my fuck'n queen... have some damn respect.... ole bitch ass nigga!" After every line, I banked him with the banger.

There was blood all over the place, but I didn't care. The circle of people that were watching had all backed up. Looks of shock, surprise and humor were on their faces.

I kicked the nigga in his face, getting blood all over my Jordan's. Then I hacked up a loogie and spit in his face.

"If it is a next time, you disrespect mine, I'll send your punk ass to say what's up to yo big brother." Then I looked over to my queen.

"Are you ready, Mama?" I asked, reaching my hand out for hers after tucking my piece back on my hip. Then I escorted her to the Charger like we were on our way to the prom.

As I walked around the car towards the driver's side, I called out to the crowd, "Hell is coming to West Oakland and the Devil's coming with it!"

It was my favorite, well one of my favorite lines from the movie, *Tombstone*. I climbed back into my whip and drove off.

"Thank you for holding me down, babe!" Tasha said as we drove away.

"You don't ever have to thank me for doing what I'm supposed to do. Ain't no nigga walking under the sun on God's green earth going to talk to you with disrespect." I was as serious as a Category 5 Tornado coming through the Midwest.

"I love you so much, Jeff. Even just being you, you are better than any other man that I know." She leaned over and kissed me on my cheek.

I brushed the compliment off and instead asked her, "Are you hungry? You want something to eat?"

"What are you talking about? You know I'm hungry," she replied with a smile.

"I was thinking Souls." That was my suggestion.

"Ooh, I could use some of their turkey wings. That sounds like a plan to me."

I changed the music that was playing to some Jill Scott and made my way to East Oakland to the restaurant. When we pulled up, the parking lot looked like they were busy. Something told me I should've called ahead, but I wasn't thinking.

"Are we eating here?" Tasha asked as we walked through the door.

I swear the place smelled heavenly. Instantly my mouth became watery.

"Naaw, babe, I got something I need to take care of. We will eat in next time."

Every time I came to Souls, one of the waitresses flirted with me. I was always nice and respectful, but I let her know that I had a woman.

With that being said, I was still praying she wasn't at work. Souls was owned by one of the local churches. All of its employees were members of the congregation. Yet, I've never seen her at any of the functions when the local churches got together, I only ran into her at the restaurant.

Thankfully, she wasn't here. Tasha and I placed our order and was pulling out of the parking lot about thirty minutes later. Tasha ate her food while I drove.

When we pulled into the projects, my cell phone rang. I looked at the caller ID before answering and saw that it was Ty.

"Dollar-Sign talk to me, I'll talk back," I answered him.

"Nigga, why you always calling me that name?" he responded.

"Because, my nigga, you about to get so much money that's all anyone is going to be calling you."

"Yeah! Yeah! I respect that!" He got excited behind this.

"But check me out, are you ready to roll?"

"Yeah, I'm dropping the wife off, as we speak. I'll be out your way in a few," I answered.

"Bet, we'a be out front waiting on you."

"Bet." I hung up.

"Make sure no matter what y'all about to do, that you think straight and y'all be careful." Tasha told me after I hung up.

84

"Say less, little mama," I told her, because what's understood ain't got to be spoken.

I walked my baby to her apartment and said hello to Ms. Carla before heading out to meet up with Ty Dollar-Sign.

When I reached the spot, Ty and the Twinz were out in the front yard posted up by their uncle's car, smoking on a Backwood full of purple Kush.

I was in a stolen car that we'd gotten earlier and left parked around the corner from the projects. When they saw me, they waited a second and scanned the block to make sure all was safe. Then they made their way to the car in preparation to get in. Even with them scanning the block, I was on point. My eyes stayed open and I kept something big and ugly on my hip ready just in case.

"What's up, Jeff To Da Left?" Ty asked, after closing the passenger door. The Twinz had already climbed into the backseat.

"Same ole shit just a different day," I answered.

The Twinz made eye contact with me through the rearview mirror and hit me with the head nod, which I returned with one of my own.

We were getting ready to hit the spot of a nigga named Troy Malone in Cypress Village. I was able to find out this nigga was the last person to see Jay alive. Troy was Jay's supplier and apparently, he'd just recently hit Jay off with a kilo. Troy wasn't originally from Cypress but a few years back, him and his Soul Strippas niggaz took over the project, on some old get-down or lay-down type of shit.

Troy and his Soul Strippas put the fear of God into everybody when they first jumped on the scene. But as the money came in, they got comfortable and grew relaxed. This is what happens with most niggaz when they sitting on a lot

of money. They should've stayed ten toes grounded and on point! Why? They wouldn't have gotten hit or what?

There was a group of niggaz hanging out in the front of the Village. I counted about ten or twelve niggaz. I drove right on by like I belonged there. A couple niggaz looked at the car but not too seriously. After all, we were all young niggaz. No one would perceive us as a threat. Stupid mothafuckas!

I checked the rearview to make sure the niggaz were still doing what they were doing and were not worried about us. When I met Kane's eyes, all I saw was death. I glanced at Abel's eyes and was confused by the humor that I saw revealed in his eyes. These little niggaz were only fourteen but were already stone-cold killers. I guess that was that Frisco City life. I couldn't reflect on it for too long, niggaz had work to do.

We found a spot to park and made our way over to the apartment unit he used as his honeycomb hideout. We came up on the information from Tony's baby mama, Yvette. It would appear that he's been fucking with her little sister for about a year and didn't realize his baby mama knew about it. Yvette was more than willing to assist us with tonight's revenge, and she assured us that there would only be two niggaz outside the unit on point.

It was dark, either the bulb had blown out or somebody unscrewed it. It wasn't uncommon to unscrew or remove the light bulbs outside. Niggaz wanted to keep shit in the dark.

*Psst*! *Psst*! *Psst*! *Psst*! *Psst*! That was the sound of the guns Ty got from his uncle, killing the two niggaz outside. Ty's uncle, Big Roc, was fucking with the largest organization in the Bay Area, the Neva Die Dragon Gang. Which made getting guns with silencers as easy as getting McDonald's hamburger and French fries.

Just as Yvette said it would be, the front door was unlocked. Kane was the first one through, followed by me, then Abel and finally Ty.

The first thing I heard was loud moans of pleasure coming from one of the back rooms. We fanned out like an army platoon and checked the entire apartment in like twenty seconds. It was empty. Except for the room with the noise.

Abel was actually licking his lips with anticipation. Kane slowly turned the knob on the door. The moans and screams covered the sound of the door hinges whining as he pushed the door open.

The smell of sex was heavy in the air. When the door opened up, the smell slapped me in the face. In front of us, Yvette was bent over in the doggy-style position, throwing that ass back like she was trying to win a prize. Troy's back was towards us. He never knew we were there until Ty spoke.

"God damn! She making that thang look better than a porn movie."

Troy froze in mid stroke.

"Don't let us stop you. I'll let you get your nutt before I bust your shit," I told him.

"What the fuck you lil niggaz want?" Troy didn't look the least bit worried or afraid.

"Since you ain't gonna finish, you can begin with sitting your mothafuck'n ass on the bed." Troy complied. The look on his face was priceless. Imagine me getting scared from a nigga mean mugging me and I am the one with the gun.

"If she is giving it to you like that, why are you fucking on her sister? Ole stupid ass nigga. Now you fucked and it's all because of some pussy." Troy looked at Ty like he suddenly grew six heads.

"Nigga, all this because of some fucking pussy?" He turned to look at Yvette. "Bitch, you set me up because I'm

fucking on your sister? Bitch, when I get up out of here, I'm going to kill you."

"Punk ass nigga, you the bitch." Yvette reached over and slapped the shit out of Troy. "That's why yo bitch ass ain't gone make it out of here, nigga."

I'm not gonna lie, for a skinny chick, Yvette had curves in all the right places. I saw them when she stood up to gather her clothes.

"Check it out. Troy, I know your family is heavy off in that voodoo shit. If you utter one word I don't understand, I'm gonna shoot you. And I'mma make sure it's some place that won't do too much damage, so we can do this shit all night." I laid the groundwork out for him.

"Where's the product, nigga?" Ty looked very uncomfortable as he asked.

When Troy looked at the Twinz, was the only time he showed some type of fear. Maybe the voodoo allowed him to see some shit on their souls that the normal eyes couldn't see.

"Brah, I'm not worried about the dope or the money. Y'all caught me slippin. Y'all can have all that shit, it's in the closet of the second room. Just stall me out one time and let a nigga breathe." I still didn't detect no fear. This nigga wasn't doing no sniveling or bitching, he was talking in his normal voice, like it was just another day at the office for him.

Ty left. No doubt to check the room and see if the shit was where he said.

"I'm not going to beat around the bush with you, Troy. I didn't come here for your dope or your money."

"Yes, young Jeff To Da Left. I know why you're here. And I swear on the blood of my dead mother, I cannot help you. I do not have the answers you seek," he spoke in a different voice. The voice was deep and trance-like, smooth, yet raspy at the same time.

"Oh, you are going to have some answers for me." For some reason I didn't feel as confident as I was acting.

When I shot him in his right kneecap, the only thing Troy did was smile a wicked smile. Twenty-five minutes later, I'd shot him four different places and tortured him something bad. No matter what I did, he still didn't make a sound.

A strange feeling overcame me. An unexplainable feeling, indescribable! I couldn't shake it. And I was still clueless, just as confused and full of questions regarding Jay, as I was when we came in.

I left Troy's apartment with ten kilos, seven coke and three heroin, and forty-nine thousand dollars, and respect for Troy. I know if I had gone through what I put him through, I probably would've been doing all kinds of whooping and hollering. Brah never said a peep.

*** **3X** ***

# CHAPTER 11

I got back home extremely late that night. From the activity level out on the street I will say, it was nearing two in the morning...

Ordinarily, I didn't like to leave Mama J. alone like that because she was taking Jay's murder extremely difficult. Lately, she has been mumbling to herself a lot and acting weird.

One night I caught her sitting in our room, talking to his closet. It broke my heart to witness her losing herself. Even though I wanted to be there for her, I didn't know how. So, I did the only sensible thing I knew and that was to hold her in my arms and fall asleep in Jay's bed.

It's gotten so bad it's become almost a nightly thing.

The sounds of her crying once again could be heard as I entered the apartment. I was as tired as a funeral worker after a long war in the hood. All I wanted to do was let my head touch the pillow and be out, Gonzo-Ponzo!

Clearly this wasn't going to happen, I guess this comes with the territory. You know, being the man of the house. I'd already told myself there was nothing I wouldn't do to make Mama J. happy.

When I entered the room, she was laying in her normal spot, crying into one of Jay's pillows. I took my pants and shirt off and climbed in bed with my boxers and a wife-beater on. I stretched my arms out and pulled her in my embrace.

"Ssssh. It's okay, Mama, I got you." I lightly kissed her on the back of her neck for reassurance.

That's the moment the unexplained happened. I got an erection. I didn't know what to do. I was so embarrassed. My heart began racing and my breath got caught in my chest. Don't get me wrong, Mama J. was beautiful. She reminded

me of a young Angela Bassett, with a body like Kimmie J. I just never looked at her in that light.

By now my shit was fully erect, and pressing hard against her ass cheeks. After finally gaining my wits back, I scooted my hips back, so we weren't touching below. That's when the second unexplained thing happened. She moaned slightly from what I guessed was frustration and pushed her hips backwards so that her ass was pressing firmly up against my cock again.

"Mmm, baby, that feels soooo good." While saying this, she began rotating her hips, so her ass was grinding against me.

What the fuck was I supposed to do? That shit was feeling hella good. My shit got even harder. I can't lie, I felt like a weasel and dirt bag. This was my dead partna's mom and here I was letting her grind her ass up against my rock-hard dick and it felt good.

I tried to protest, but she took my hand and placed it on one of her breasts and manipulated it to start massaging her breast.

"Mmm, Jay, don't stop please. Mommy is broken and I need you to help me. I haven't been with a man since Daddy left. Everyone always leaves Mommy. First my parents, then Daddy and now you. Everyone always leaves me because I'm ugly. Jay, I need you to show me I'm beautiful. Show me you won't leave me. That you haven't left." Her ass was moving faster now with more purpose.

I was breathless and speechless. I didn't know what to say. I didn't trust myself anyway at that moment. My voice could have possibly betrayed the fact that I was loving that shit.

"H-h-how, Mama? W-what do you want me to do?" I somehow managed to get out.

"Mmm… touch me, baby. Touch Mommy," she begged me.

What can I say? I complied. Her skin was velvety soft and hot. I began rubbing all over her body.

"Sssss. Yeessss." The moans gave testament to our debauchery.

She reached back between us and grabbed my cock. When she squeezed it, it was my turn to moan.

Suddenly, the reality of what we were doing became clear to me. Not only was this shit taboo as fuck, it was wrong on so many levels. It was beyond dirty.

What if she really wasn't aware of her actions? How would she look at me then? I was not only her son's best friend. I was her godson. What kind of nigga was I to take advantage of her? Thinking about protecting her from herself, I bolted out of the bed like lightning, into Jay's room and climbed in the bed.

Her sobs began again, but this time they were louder. "No one loves me. I'm going to die alone because I'm so ugly." She cried hard as ever.

Her cries turned to moans. It sounded like she was masturbating. What the fuck was going on?

The noises turned me on. I had a hard dick and a fucked-up conscience. I started jacking off, fantasizing about how good it would feel to have gone all the way and had sex with her.

*** **3X** ***

**Mama J.**

by the size of Jeffrey's penis. Dear Lord, to receive it is going to be a blessing. I laid in Jay's bed that night, imagining what it's going to feel like to have something so massive invading my sweet love tunnel.

*** **3X** ***

When I awakened the next morning, it was truly to a heavenly bliss one could only feel on earth. Jeffrey was already up and out of the house by then. This is one of the reasons it is taking me so long to get him to make love to me. I haven't had a chance to sit him down and talk to him.

I got dressed listening to Marvin Sapp's song as he told someone how he never would've made it, if it had not been for them. Tell me he wasn't talking to our heavenly father!

After today's message, Reverend Jacobs pulled me to the side to see how I was doing. I spoke with the good Reverend for about twenty minutes just out of respect. Because the good reverend was full of crap. No matter what we were discussing, the reverend would find some type of way to come on to me. Now that was the worst kind of blasphemy.

When I got home, Jeffrey was gone, as always. I walked straight to my room, got undressed and stepped into the shower. Since I was alone, I didn't bother about closing the door. I've never been a fan of steamy bathrooms. I always preferred the door open or the window.

Just as I was preparing to get out of the shower, I heard Jeffrey come into the apartment. My pulse quickened. It was either "Now or never," I told myself. Thinking quickly, I hid my body wash.

"Jeffrey! Baby, could you give Mama a hand, sweetie?" I called out as loud as needed for him to hear me.

"What you need, Mama J.?" He was so respectable that he didn't even walk past the threshold.

"Can you hand me one of them bars of Caress Silk out of the drawer please, baby?" I used the sweetest voice I could muster up. Look at me, playing the role of the Wicked Witch in the story, *Snow White*. I was about to seduce this young boy out of his innocence.

He walked into the bathroom with his head turned away from the slower. For a second, I thought my attempt would go in vain, until I caught him looking at my body in the mirror. The revelation that he was interested went stirring through my body, beginning at my vagina.

As he opened the drawer to retrieve the soap, I opened the shower door all the way. Jeff turned around, saw my full naked body and froze in his tracks. He was so stunned that he dropped the box containing the bar of soap.

"It's okay, baby. All it is, is God's purity in its natural form. There's nothing to be ashamed of. Look at me, Jeffrey." The last part I spoke like a coach coaching his MVP player along, at half-time of a Super Bowl or the NBA Championship.

Slowly he turned in my direction. The moment he did, the first thing I saw was his massive erection straining against the fabric of his jeans. He picked up the box of soap, opened it and took out the bar of soap. Next, he reached his hand out with the soap in it for me to take.

I could see the lust in his eyes. Although he was trying his hardest to cover it, I could see it just below the surface, waiting to be freed.

"Could you be a dear and wash Mama's back for her, baby?" I could tell I was going to have to guide him, which was fine with me. Yes, it was!

"I-I, O…" He was too cute with his shy self.

"It's okay, baby," I told him as I put my loofah in his hand, leaving him no other option.

"O-Okay." Those were the words I was dying to hear.

Attentively, he began to wash across the top of my shoulders. My entire body exploded into a tingling of warm, delicious nerves.

I lifted my left hand towards the nozzle spray. This caused the water to spray over my head, getting Jeffrey wet.

"Oooh, I'm sorry, honey." I feigned innocence. Somehow, I maintained my innocence even after it happened two more times. "Jeffrey, Sweetie, why don't you take your nice clothes off, they are getting all wet."

"I-It's ok..." The water spraying in his face cut off his words.

"Ooh Baby, I'm sorry. Let me help you." I turned around to face him and began lifting his shirt over his head.

*** 3X ***

## JEFF TO DA LEFT

Last night was crazy insane. To try and better understand it, I wrote it off as Mama J. being in a bad state of mind.

I don't understand the woman that has basically raised me as my foster mom, trying to give me the pussy!

I would've been cool if it stopped there. When I walked into the apartment that Sunday, all bets went out the window.

The moment she called me into the back room, I didn't think twice about it. Just being honest, my conscience was "out to lunch." When she asked me to grab the soap, I turned my head to look away from the shower, trying to keep it G.

What the fuck was I supposed to do when I saw all of her beautiful nakedness through the mirror? Mama J. was stacked!

At that moment, I realized she wasn't as thick as Kimmie J. Mama J. was fucking over Kimmie J! It wasn't my fault my dick came to life!

Don't get me wrong, I was madly in love with Tasha. I still am. But looking at Mama J.'s body, Tasha didn't exist at the moment. A man was going to be a man. And with all this pussy in front of me, I had to taste it.

Hell, when I turned around with the box of soap in my hand, I almost shitted on myself. Looking at her through glass was one thing, but for her body to be displayed directly in plain sight all wet and soaped up was another.

Fuck that!

God had to know what I was going to do. I know he did, because I heard the Devil when he told me to do it and I know God hears everything. I didn't care if it was wrong, it was worth it.

I found myself standing behind her in my boxer briefs, washing her back. My dick was hurting, it was so hard. I couldn't help but wonder how it would feel to bend her over right there in the shower and beat her pussy up.

"Mmmm, thank you, baby. Make sure to wash my lower back, baby." Her head was hanging low and she slowly rocked back and forth. The water cascaded down her voluptuous body.

I couldn't take it no more. I released my dick through the pee hole of my boxers and began stroking it. The sight of my dick so close to her giant booty drove me crazy. Before I knew it, I'd stopped washing her back and was vigorously beating my dick. In my head, I was picturing my dick sliding in and out of her hitting it doggy style, disappearing between those humongous ass cheeks.

"Umm… Jeffrey, honey?" This brought me out of my trance. "What are you doing back there?" There was humor in her voice, but I was still scared like a thief caught in the act.

I paused, frozen mid-stroke, with my dick pulsating in my grip.

She turned around. "Are you masturbating, Jeffrey?" I was speechless. I was so embarrassed she had caught me. "Let me help you." She licked her lips and reached down and took my dick out of my hand before I could react.

The water bouncing off her body and splashing into my face was the only proof I had that I wasn't dreaming. Her touch was heavenly, even though our act was forbidden. When she leaned in to kiss me, her hardened nipples felt like tiny bullets shooting into the armor of my resolve.

Just when I thought things couldn't get any better, she kissed me deeply and sensually on the lips. Her hot mouth had a watermelon flavor to it from the remainder of lip gloss she was wearing. This kiss was heating up. My dick jumped in her hand, reminding her not to forget about it. She didn't! To my surprise, she got down on her knees and took me into her mouth. At that moment, the Devil really had me. I was no longer in control, the Devil had taken over me. Instead of staying timid or getting more embarrassed, all the "G" came out of me.

"That's right, make sure you suck that dick good now!" I guess she was shocked because she cut her eyes up at me.

But if that surprised her, my next words fucked her up!

"Don't look at me, bitch! Watch that dick as you swallow it!" That must've turned her on, because she began sucking the shit out of my dick. Her head moved back and forth at a rapid pace.

I watched in amazement as my dick disappeared beyond her lips and into her mouth. The shit drove me absolutely, fucking crazy.

I stopped her before I came, suggesting that we take what we started and finish in the bedroom. Fuck it! There was no turning back now. I followed her as we made our way out of the bathroom and into the room, watching the cheeks of her ass as they bounced with each step. I love a nice, big ole booty!

"I like when you talk to me like that, Jeffrey." Mama J. sounded like a scary schoolgirl.

"Then shut your ass up and climb on that bed so I can taste that pretty pussy. I know that mothafucka is sweet." She did as I commanded, giggling as she climbed on the bed. She then laid back, bent her legs and opened wide, making sure I had full access to the pussy.

Besides Mama J.'s, I had only seen two pussies. One was a toss-up and the other was Tasha's. Both Tasha and the toss-up had pretty little pussies, but Mama J.'s was beautiful. She had the largest clitoris I'd ever seen, with nice thick pussy lips. The two outer lips reminded me of butterfly wings. My tongue slid lightly across each one of her lips, causing her to inhale deeply. Next, I took her clitoris into my mouth and sucked it like a finger with honey on it.

Thanks to Tasha and our teen sexcapades, I was a pro at eating pussy.

"Mmm… Jeffrey, baby, that feels so good. Make Mama feel good, baby," she cried out.

I let my tongue lay flat up against her lips and licked my way upwards. When I got back to her clit, I kissed it and sucked it into my mouth. My hands were rubbing every inch of her naked flesh, exploring places I could only feel before in the confines of my fantasies. I sucked her clit in between my

lips as hard as I could, while the tip of my tongue played freeze tag with it.

"Oh my God, Jeffrey! Oh my God, right there. Yes! Yes! Make Mama cum, baby!" Her hips were rocking violently as she bucked against my face and palmed the back of my head.

I held on like a bull-riding cowboy. When she came, she shot streams all over the place like a water hose. I rode the waves of pleasure with her, still sucking on my forbidden passion fruit while gripping her ass cheeks. When she was done bucking, she gushed in my mouth and there was a puddle of her love juice under her. I knew very well what a gusher was from watching porn videos on *XNXX.com*.

I rubbed my hand in the puddle, getting my fingers nice and wet. Before she knew what I was doing, my middle finger was knuckle-deep in her asshole.

"N-no…no J-Jeffrey, not in Mama's butt," she pleaded with me.

"Shit up, bitch, and cum in my face again! Fuck my finger with your ass!" I was ramming my finger in and out of her ass while I was instructing her.

"O-O-Oh…Ooooh! Okay! Okay! Fuck my ass, baby, fuck it!" she howled out as my fist smacked over and over against her ass cheeks, while my finger crammed in her hole.

With my tongue and lips still on her clit, it wasn't long after she was coming again. This time she erupted like a volcano. Screaming my name over and over. I didn't wait out her spasms. I climbed on top and rode 'em out with her. Her walls were tight. Yet their attempts at preventing my invasion were futile. Her pussy was way too slippery for that. I slid balls deep into her and grinded until the waves of her orgasm subsided. Then I began a slow stroke that drove her crazy.

She kept shaking her head and screaming, "Oh, my God! Jeffrey, you're loving Mama so good. Yes baby, show Mama you love her. Fuck me, baby!"

She didn't have to worry or wait. I was eager to comply. Deep, slow strokes gave way to hard, fast, deep strokes. I was power driving into her over and over, over and over, pounding harder and harder!

I felt her walls constricting, letting me know she was on the brink of another orgasm. I wrapped my arms around the bottom of her thighs and jack-knifed them high in the air.

That move gave me full access! I drove nine inches deep, thrust after powerful thrust, deep into that pussy!

"Ooooh J-Jeffrey, I-I feel a big one.... Ssss give it to meeeee!" She erupted again!

I felt myself not far behind. I pulled out of her and erupted on her stomach. I sprayed so much, it literally covered half of her stomach.

I collapsed onto her. We laid like that for a good five minutes before getting in the shower, where we had round two. We crossed a forbidden line of passion but for some reason, I didn't care. For some strange, twisted reason, it felt natural.

*** **3X** ***

# CHAPTER 12

## TY DOLLAR-SIGN

God damn! Some good pussy is one of the hardest things for a nigga to walk away from. Dasia had some knock 'em down, die hard, kill yo best friend pussy. Dasia was this side-piece I fucked from time to time, because the pussy was fire.

A nigga damn near wanted to say fuck leaving and stay with the pussy, but a nigga had that work to do. That money to make! Couldn't be Ty Dollar-Sign if I wasn't making that paper. Everybody has a position to play on a team and I fa'sho was 'bout to play mine to the fullest.

That little lick that we hit the other day was exactly what the doctor ordered. While Jay was doing his A-Team thing, I was playing the backfield watching, learning and waiting. My time playing the backfield allowed me the opportunity to meet a lot of niggaz and get my networking on. Niggaz were not only hungry but had a vision.

It was unfortunate when Jay was murdered, because he and I were getting ready to make our move. He had all the important connections, and I had the clientele. His murder slowed things down, but I made some rearrangements.

I was driving down W. Grand Avenue, on my way to the California Hotel. I had two people waiting on me to drop them a bundle so they could get started. I'd give each one four, thousand-count bundles. Three of them were mine that they needed to sell, in order for the fourth one to be theirs.

"Aye yo, call that nigga Jamal first and tell that fool to come on down," I told Abel, who was sitting in the back seat.

I don't allow anyone but Jeff To Da Left and the Twinz to sit behind me. Too many niggaz have been betrayed and died that way.

I saw Jamal coming out of the building just as we were pulling up.

"Dollar-Sign, what it do, baby?" he greeted me as he climbed inside the whip.

Everyone already knew it was a waste of time greeting either of the Twinz. They didn't talk much, but when it was time to handle their business, they let their guns do their talking.

"You know me, baby, chasing the American Dream," I answered.

Jamal was from Cypress Village originally. In his days, he was an Oakland elite. He had broken the Golden Rule and let a bitch trick him into getting high on his own shit. He still had major hustle in him, only he didn't want the riches any longer. Now he hustled for the high.

He would smoke up the majority of his own pack. I wasn't sweating it. As long as my count was always right. My uncle, Big Roc turned me on to Jamal. Roc was now linked with a heavy organization, the Neva Die Dragon Gang. They'd taken over all of the major drug sales in the Bay Area. If you were selling dope, nine times out of ten, it came from them.

Now that Roc was in the Big Leagues, I had free reign over his old clientele.

If the stories were true, Jamal had watched Big Roc kill both of his parents as a lesson never to play with him or his money. I don't believe every rumor that I hear. But if it is true, I don't have to worry about the nigga fucking up my count.

"How long do you think you are gonna need on this?" I questioned him as I handed him the package. I needed to make sure I didn't leave any room for error. In my eyes, the mothafucka was still a smoker.

"Shit man, if this shit's as good as you say, I'll be ready for you in about a couple of days. Shit, three tops." The way he was looking at the packages I could tell he wanted me to shut the fuck up so he could go get high.

This was my first time dealing with Blood on this level. I didn't give a fuck about nothing but making sure we were crystal clear about my money.

"Aaight! Hit me when you need me." The nigga damn near broke his neck getting out the car.

He got out in front of the California Hotel, which was a gold mine. It was one of those places that would give smokers and homeless people a room, free of charge for most, fifteen dollars a day for others. The government paid the rent under some special program or something.

The thing is, the mothafucka had five hundred rooms. Picture this, ten floors with fifty rooms on each floor, with all smokers and ex-smokers. And since they were allowed to have visitors, on any given day, you could have over a thousand dope fiends in one spot. Not to mention, you didn't have to worry about the police.

A fucking gold-mine!

Paradise was coming out of the building as Jamal was getting out of the car. Paradise has sold dope for me long enough to know the routine and we had an understanding, so I didn't have to tell her shit.

I pulled away from the curb and drove over to Taco Bell on San Pablo. I did this in case somebody was watching a nigga. Shit would look funny if both of them climbed into my shit and left carrying a bag. I let Paradise buy whatever she wanted as long as she asked for an extra bag. I put the work in the empty bag. When I pulled back in front of the hotel, it looked like I gave her a ride to Taco Bell.

After dropping her off, I made my way over to Ghost Town to meet up with my mans. I don't know about the rest of the hustlahs out there, but I was getting that early morning money. I was the early bird getting the worm.

My cell phone started ringing as I was driving up Telegraph Street. The caller ID let me know that it was Jeff To Da Left.

"Speak to me, soldier. You're on speaker, it's just Abel and me in the car." I turned the volume down on the stereo.

"What's up, fam? I'm just tapping in making sure shit is copasetic. Shit, I had a wild night, last night. I'm talking oversleep on the first day of work, kind of night."

"Nigga, let me find out you down at the church house tricking with them little old ladies," I joked into the phone.

"Nigga, you know I'm not with that kissing and telling. But you better believe I'm not fucking with the church like that. Anyway, I'mma meet y'all up at the trap in a couple of hours," Jeff To Da Left told me.

That was cool with a nigga like me, cause Abel and I still had some drops to make.

"Aaight, bet that!" I responded, before hanging up the phone.

I continued to make my rounds throughout the West. I was a couple of hours already into my drop-off. More cars were on the road now, as more mothafuckas were waking up and heading to work.

Since I was already over by KIPP Bridge Academy, I decided to swing by my baby mama crib. Tiesha was a good mama to my two-year-old daughter, Stephanie. She was also two years older than me, but she carried herself like a grown woman in her late twenties.

Tiesha was five-eleven and weighed close to one-forty. She was what we called in the hood, a slim goody. Although she was petite, she had the right kinds of curves in all the right places. She always reminded a nigga of that old school *Jason's Lyric,* Jada Pinkett, before she added the Smith to it.

When I turned down Myrtle Street, the first thing I saw was a crowd out front of her house. Wasn't no telling what was going on, because my baby mama was always doing too much. She was always extra'd the fuck out.

I looked at the little homie in the rearview. The look on his face told me all I needed to do was push the button on his battery pack. I pulled up and both of us hopped out the whip, turnt the fuck up and ready for whatever.

No sooner did we start to part the crowd, I heard that bitch ass nigga she fucks with. Some bitch ass nigga named Ugz from East Palo Alto.

"Bitch, you think I'm stupid? I told you about having that bitch ass nigga over here." He was yelling at Tiesha, while beating the dog shit out of her.

Now her getting her ass beat wasn't my concern. But I done told that nigga about putting his hands on her in front of my daughter, who was standing in the doorway crying and shaking violently from fear. Plus, I know this nigga didn't call me a bitch.

"Ugz, he is my daughter's father. What am I supposed to do, tell him he can't see his daughter?"

*SLAP*!

He slapped her so hard, I felt it.

"Bitch, don't you be talking to me like shit is sweet over here!" He reached his hand back and slapped the fire from her face.

Seeing it made my blood boil.

"Bitch, you better tell that nigga that shit ain't a game over here!" He slapped her again for good measure.

The Desert Eagle came off my hip, ready to fly in any direction I pointed.

"Nah! You ole pussy ass nigga, why don't you tell me!" When the bystanders and onlookers saw two feet of chrome in my hand, they parted ways like Moses was in this bitch. They backed up a good five feet or so.

We were fully in the front yard now. The chain link fence acted like the hexagon fighting cage in the UFC.

Ugz turned around. He was a lanky nigga. If I had to guess, I'd say he was about six-three or six-four and skinny as shit. But he was one of them high-yellow pretty ass niggaz. So, he stayed in another niggaz' bitches faces dirty Mackn'n and trying to get some pussy.

Not only was he soft as fuck, but he was also snitching on niggaz. The word on the street was he'd already taken down four niggaz.

"M-man... T-Ty, this ain't got nothing to do with you, rogue." The nigga went from He-Man to Mrs. Doubtfire instantaneously.

"Naaw... naaw, pussy, let me hear that message you got for me." As calm as I was talking, a smart man would've known a storm was indeed coming.

"M-man, it's just that..."

*WHAM!*

I am only five-eleven, but the barrel of the Desert Eagle evened the height difference as I knocked that bitch upside his head! He stumbled backwards and tripped over his own feet.

I turned towards Tiesha. "Get up and take my daughter in her room. A child shouldn't see grown-up shit."

"Daddy," my baby cried out.

"Daddy will be there in a minute, princess. Go with Mommy and tell her she is beautiful." Seeing my princess instantly took this fire out of me. That is, until I remembered what she was witnessing when I pulled up.

When I turned around and looked down at Ugz, he was cowering down, looking up at me like a defeated fighter who knew he'd already lost.

"T-T-Ty-Ty, let's talk 'bout this shit like men," he pleaded.

"Bitch ass nigga. Did you let my baby mom's talk about it?" When he tried to respond, I attacked like a rabid, red nose Pitbull.

*Wham! Wham! Wham!*

I was going crazy. The side of his head caved in from the blows of the pistol. Here I was, pistol whipping a nigga to death in front of the entire neighborhood. I didn't give a fuck! Niggaz needed to know that Gas Nation wasn't playing no games with no fuck niggaz. Revenge really was Promised!

Gasping for breath and dripping sweat, I finally stopped. Then I knelt down in front of him. He was barely conscious, and his entire face was covered in blood.

"Since you like running your fucking mouth, open up, bitch!" I forced the cold chrome barrel into his mouth. "Bitch, suck on this barrel like you wanna live."

"Mmm, mmm, mmm," he was begging to say something.

I pulled the Desert Eagle out his mouth.

"C-come on, T-Ty. I'm sorry, rogue. Don't do me like this!" This nigga actually was crying I'm talking about crocodile tears and snot running down his nose

"Bitch, either suck it or start praying!" I meant every word I was saying.

I forced the chrome back in his mouth. I'll be damned! I really didn't think he would do it. Ugz started sucking the barrel of the Desert Eagle like it was a real-life dick.

The crowd was ooohing and aaaahing, watching this fuck nigga suck on a chrome dick.

He was sucking so hard that the scene turned gay.

*BOOM*!

Right there in front of God, Moses, the neighborhood and some more niggaz, I ended it all by blowing his mothafuck'n head off!

The force off the blow knocked him back to the ground. The crowd was shocked.

"RIP nigga, fucking with Gas Nation Revenge Is Promised, nigga!" I called out.

Abel had a grin on his face when I looked at him.

"Get rid of the body and the whip. I'mma stick around in case the police come and make sure everybody out here got amnesia," I spoke loud enough for everyone to hear me. "Swoop back in a couple of hours and come get me."

After giving Abel his orders, I walked in the house to tend to my baby's mother and my princess.

**\*\*\* 3X \*\*\***

# CHAPTER 13

## JEFF TO DA LEFT

Word about what Ty did to the nigga Ugz spread throughout the West like a wildfire in Southern California. It didn't do anything but add to the buzz that Gas Nation was already creating. Mothafuckas knew not to fuck with us. By now we had three trap spots. One was in Acorn, one in the Lower Bottoms and one in the Alphabets. We were starting to see some paper, which added to our buzz.

Pretty soon, the numbers of our ranks began to expand. Since Kane and Abel didn't want to be trap gods, they each led a hit squad of young niggaz. Some from Oakland and some from San Francisco. All loyal only to them.

Therefore, I outsourced. Tasha's older brother, Aubrey, ran the trap in the Alphabets. I reached out to Margo's brother, Sean, to run the Acorn Trap, while Ty Dollar-Sign still took care of the Lower Bottoms trap.

I was over in the Lower Bottoms, messing with Ty Dollar-Sign. We were just going over a few ideas that he and I had in our heads. Although I wanted the niggaz that killed Jay something fierce. I knew it would take patience, and in the meantime, we had a team to lead and a building trap squad to run.

"Bruh think about that shit. What in the fuck are we going to do with a clique of women?" Ty was just proposing that we allowed a female unit of Gas Nation.

"You're not seeing this shit right, Blood. Bitches will be perfect! A team of bitches that can go where niggaz can't, who got the know on how niggaz move. Blood, that's priceless. I'm telling you, To Da Left, we can't sleep on this. These bitches are prime and ready. If we don't snatch 'em up, somebody's

gonna and we're gonna be fucked." As adamant as he was about this, I was willing to consider it.

As I was getting ready to tell him that, I spotted an all-white painter's van creeping slowly up the street about five houses down.

"What's up with Blood?" I called out to Ty at the same time as I was coming off of the hips with twin .40's. Wasn't any need to cock them because they already were.

No sooner did I come up off the hammers, did the van speed up. When the passenger window rolled down and the sliding door rolled back, I was ready.

*BOCCA! BOCCA! BOCCA!*

*Thaatat! Thaatat! Thaatat!*

The van screeched to a stop directly in front of the house and we lit the night up like the New Year Eve's celebration.

Ty dove to his left just before a line of bullets chewed up the ground where he just was. The mothafuckas in the van were spraying bullets from automatics, which sounded like TEC-9's.

I couldn't afford to move. Fuck around and run right into a bullet. Instead I held my ground. Bussing like a hillbilly protecting his farm.

*BOOM! BOOM! BOOM!* The sound of Ty's big .45 rang out.

The passenger's head snapped back like he was cracked with a baseball bat. The blood, bone fragments and brain matter that sprayed out the back of his head was testament that a bullet crashed into his face. Immediately, the driver peeled off. The nigga shooting out the sliding door kept letting that thang bang!

I ran out of the yard, chasing the van, letting both .40's bang out as well. Once the van turned the corner, I turned

back to the trap ready to act a donkey. None of those little niggaz inside of the trap had come outside. Fa'sho I was about to kill them.

Ty was wiping the dirt off his clothes when I walked back inside the yard. But I wasn't paying attention to none of that. Little Omarion was sprawled out on the porch with a huge puddle of blood under him. At least he was accounted for. He died like a soldier was supposed to. I walked up to the porch ignoring the smell of gunpowder, blood and shit, which confirmed Omarion was dead. I saluted the dead body and stepped over the fallen soldier.

Ty followed me inside the trap. All my questions were answered. Duke and Dave were both dead as fuck. Duke was on the floor. It looked like he was trying to get to the front door. Dave was still seated at the table, with his head bowed laying in a pool of blood.

"Get the money, brah, I'll grab the work," Ty called out.

We had to get up out of there fast before Oakland P.D. showed up. Within a couple of minutes, we were out of the spot and in Ty's Durango, headed towards Acorn Projects.

"Brah, who the fuck was that?" Ty called out as he maneuvered through the back streets.

"I don't know, but we need to find out. The way they just got at us is like we some bitches or something. Whatever it is, it's not about to stop." I was pissed the fuck off.

'You already know, To Da Left, R.I.P."

"R.I.P.," I repeated. Niggaz were stupid if they didn't believe Revenge Is Promised.

I pulled out my cell and sent the Twinz a message to come over to the Acorns ASAP. When we pulled up to the projects, I instructed Ty to pull to the back. Our visual would be cut off, but no one was stupid enough to come close to the back of The Corns (as we called the projects) and expect to make it out.

The Twinz came rolling up about five minutes after we pulled into the projects.

"To Da Left! What's up wit Blood?" Kane called out the moment he jumped out the whip. Kane was one of them dudes that was trained to go. It didn't take much for him to turn up.

Normally, Abel was the hyphy one. The one turnt up. I started to run them down what happened, but I didn't need to. They had already heard, which is why Kane was turned up.

"Look. I want the word out there now! I want to know where this came from before the night is over. For y'all to find out the way you did, means the streets are already talking. And if we don't clap back, they're going to be talking about us." The Twinz were nodding their approval of my fire.

They were ready to go!

"Fuck that. We're starting to get money, so let's act like it. We got ten bands for anybody who can tell us who the fuck that was," Ty spoke up for the first time.

"Yeah, I'm feeling that. That's some boss shit," Abel cosigned.

Y'all think ten is enough?" I wasn't questioning Ty. It's just if we were going to do it, we might as well as do it right.

"For something like this, hell yeah, ten bands is enough. It's only for some info. I'm telling you by morning we'll be ready to move on some shit." Ty assured me confidently.

"Aaight then, that's what it is then. Let's meet up on Myrtle first thing in the morning." I was ready to call it a night.

"Bet that." Abel and Kane both gave me a dap, before jumping back in Kane's all black Tahoe.

When they pulled off, I turned to Ty. "Blood, does Tiesha's people still got the line on them thangs?"

One of her people were plugged in with some niggaz from Richmond that had a line on guns. Not just basic shit either, I'm talking military edition shit.

"I think I'mma shoot through her shit tonight and find out. I'll let you know in the morning," e answered me.

"Yeah because it sounded like them niggaz were playing with TEC-9's or MAC-10's or something. It's time for us to step our weight up."

I gave my right hand the single arm gangsta hug and made my way to the apartment.

*** **3X** ***

When I walk in the door, the smell of Cherry Blossoms body spray sensually assaulted my nostrils. The sounds of Keith Sweat's "Nobody" played softly on the back speakers.

"Who could love you like me/ Nobody/ and who can give you what you need/Nobody/ and who can freak you all night all long/ Nobody baby."

That nigga Keith Sweat was making it sound good, but my stamina was pretty up to par. I was in the "Up All Night Club" too.

"And the band keeps playing on." Mama J. came slowly walking her sexy ass into the living room, wearing nothing but some high heels and a drop-dead smile.

I don't know whether it was the singing or the walking that was causing her large breasts to rise and fall, but I was loving the show, so it really didn't matter.

"I've been waiting for you to come home, Jeffrey, so you could make Mama feel good, like only you can." She stood about five-seven and weighed maybe a hundred and fifty pounds. Her only weight was in her ass and tits. C-cups, maybe a forty-two, with a forty-seven-inch ass. It's a wonder

how her little frame could hold all of that. Mama J. walked directly up to me. The look in her eyes confirmed she was lust craved. The moment she was directly in front of me, she got down on her knees.

My initial response was to prevent her from doing what I knew she was about to do. I just couldn't bring myself to do it.

Her mouth was hot and wet. Steamy like Hell's Kitchen but felt like heaven. As she sucked on me, I closed my eyes and leaned my head backwards. I can't lie. I used my right arm and palmed the back of my dead homeboy's mama's head, while she sucked my dick like Karrine "Superhead" Steffans.

The only audible sounds in the apartment, other than Keith Sweat, was the sounds of her loud moans and slurps. It was driving me crazy. When I looked down at her, she was fucking herself with three fingers. Going in and out repeatedly over and over, as fast as she could.

My sacks swelled. My stomach tightened. I was getting ready to blow like that big volcano in Hawaii.

"Come on, baby. It's okay cum in Mama's mouth." I don't know how she knew it was coming, but that shit she said guaranteed it came. I grabbed her head with both hands and pumped into her mouth. When I exploded, she gripped my ass cheeks and held me deep in her mouth. My semen shot to the back of her throat in powerful streams. After she swallowed all of it, she led me to the shower. We took turns washing each other and teasing one another before finally climbing into bed.

*** 3X ***

# CHAPTER 14

## Mama J.

From my bedroom window, I could see the back parking lot of the complex. I was just getting out of the shower when I heard Jeffrey and Tyrone pull up.

I was going to call down to him in order to trick him into somehow coming in so that I could seduce him. However, I could sense that something was wrong by their body language. A few moments later, when the other two boys pulled up, it confirmed my suspicions.

My heart raced with worry as I looked down on the boys. When worry got the best of me, I said a prayer to the mighty Jesus. Next, I slowly opened my bedroom window. Just as I had hoped, the night was so quiet, I could hear enough of their conversation. I gripped my chest from the anxiety from hearing just how close these boys came to losing their lives tonight. As much as I wanted to keep listening, I just couldn't.

I pulled myself away from the window and turned on my music playlist. I was trying to take my mind off of the bad images that played in it. I don't know how long I sat on my bed calming myself down with prayer. However long it was, I was getting ready to stand up and go to the kitchen to make a cup of tea, when the front door opened.

The timing could not have been more perfect. I'd just begun to mentally relax. Keith Sweat was singing his timeless wonder, "Nobody," which allowed my mind to travel back to "my secret garden," my place of forbidden pleasures and erotic fantasies. At the sight of Jeffrey, my sex flower blossomed to life. My petals tingled as thoughts of the other night came to mind.

"I've been waiting for you to come home, Jeffrey, so you could make Mama feel good like only you can." I didn't wait to receive a response from him.

Mama was much too confident for that. I boldly walked up to him, dropped down to my knees and pulled out his already enlarged and proliferated penis. My tingling grew just at the sight of it. I licked around the engorged head, we both shuddered. His taste was dazzling to my taste buds. My body temperature rose a few degrees. I licked my lips in preparation, then took as much of him as I could into my mouth.

Before I knew it, my fingers found their way to my newly waxed vaginal lips. My lust level was a category 5. With my fingers, I fucked myself while I sucked him. His moans encouraged my performance, elevating my arousal level. I could feel my orgasm building. Jeffrey began humping my face as I sucked him. When I felt his thrust become sporadic, I knew my reward was coming.

"Come on, baby. It's okay. Cum in Mama's mouth." A little encouragement was all it took.

He exploded a strong stream of hot, milky satisfaction to the back of my mouth. I grabbed his ass and forced his cock as deep as it would go into my mouth and held him there. The sensation of his hot cum coasting down my throat sent me over the edge. I came without touching myself.

After I made sure to swallow all of his semen, I stood up and led him to the shower. We washed the day's problems away and touched each other endlessly. Ten minutes later, we were climbing into bed. I was trying to remain in control, but I could feel her coming out of me. My alter ego. A sex-crazed lunatic.

"Now Jeffrey, get your little fine ass down here and eat Mama's sweet pussy!" He didn't have to be told twice.

Inside of me, the lady was still there, but outside of me, the freak was in control. She grabbed the back of his head and began bucking against his face.

"Unh. Unh. Yes, that's it. Eat Mama's pussy, Jeffrey!" My moans increased as I grinded into his face.

When my orgasm began building, it was tantalizingly delicious. Jeffrey's tongue attacked my clit. Alternating from making circles around it to staking the tip with dart-like precision and the swiftness of an Olympic track star. There was no way he was a beginner. Not with his skills.

I came with a heart-shattering, mind-blowing orgasm that made me see stars, a sistah exploded! The entire time I was riding the waves of pleasure, my pelvis was grinding into his face. Once I recovered, Jeffrey climbed up and gave me a sample of my sweetness with a slow, sensual kiss. My taste on his tongue was like an aphrodisiac. It drove me crazy with lust.

I directed Jeffrey to lie on his back. When he did, I climbed on top of him and straddled his hips. Our eyes met with hunger in them.

"Do you wanna fuck me, Jeffrey? Do you want to feel your cock deep inside this pussy?" I loved when my alter ego talked nasty to him. The sound was foreign to my ears as if the voice wasn't mine at all.

"Yeah, Mama J., you know I want to feel the inside of that sweet, wet pussy," he answered in a lust-filled voice.

"Then tell me," I challenged.

"Take this dick, Mama J. I want you to ride it and make me cum deep inside of that pussy." His voice was like a growl.

I leaned down and traced his lips with my tongue. He tried to trap my tongue with his lips, but I evaded his lips. I could sense his breathing getting shallower. I reached down between

us and took him into my hands. His swollen shaft filled my grasp completely. I stroked him twice before raising my hips and positioning him at the main gate of my garden.

Slowly, I slid down on his shaft. My walls stretched to their limits. "Sssss, mmmm," was all I could get out as it felt like he would never end.

Once I was sitting all the way down on his shaft, I waited a couple of seconds while my walls relaxed around him. Slowly, I rose all the way back up. At the top, I paused before slamming hard down onto it. "Ungh. Uhgh" I repeated the move over and over. The pain was lusciously delightful. I began a course of sliding up and down my stallion and rocking my hips. "Oh yeah! Grab my ass and fuck me, Jeffrey. Ungh-huh, that's it. Give Mama that dick." I was so wet, every time I bounced, our flesh would smack into each other.

He was a very good student. Right away, he gripped both sides of my ass and began thrusting upwards to meet me on the downward side of my bounce. "Ungh…. Take this dick, Mama…. aargh, come on! Get this dick!" he growled. At the same time, he spanked me.

"Ooooh Jeffrey, yes! That's right, motherfucker! That's right… fuck me. Fuck me! Ungh...fuck Mama…"

We were at it so hard that the headboard of my bed was clashing up against the wall. Then when Jeffrey raised up and sucked one of my breasts into his mouth, I lost it.

"Oooh fuck! I'm cumming, baby. Ooooh yes, suck Mama's tit."

I was bucking like a wild mare in heat. Slamming my body down on his young, hard body with no regard. Within moments, he shook violently and came deep inside of me, the both of us continuously bucking like we were in a rodeo.

We rode until the ride was over. When it was, I climbed off of him and sucked him back in my mouth. Our two tastes mixed together nicely, creating such a blissful flavor. This was merely the beginning of a long sex-filled night.

I slept in late the next day. After the long night with my young stud, I needed it. Considering it was choir practice today, sleeping in was okay, because it was my lazy day. I laid in bed all day long, daydreaming about Jeffrey and our forbidden secret. Dear Lord Jesus, that boy was doing something to me that wasn't right.

I knew if people found out, I'd be judged cruelly. But where were the judges and critics when my innocence was being stolen from me? I didn't complain and turn my back on society. Society turned its big, ugly back against me. When it did, I took it to Jesus.

"You did not create me to worry / You did not create me to fear / You created me to worship..." Our choir sang beautifully. The words of the song were personally coming from my crying soul. They brought me out of my head and out of my feelings.

The Reverend sat at the bottom of the congregation pit and watched us as we rehearsed. This made everyone sing at their Sunday Morning's best. I always wanted to do my best for the Lord, not for the reverend.

We rehearsed the seven songs we were going to sing this Sunday. After rehearsal, the reverend wanted to have a word with me, but I couldn't do it. I'd already decided that I was going to cook a good home cooked meal tonight. And I needed to swing by Safeway to pick a couple of things up. Nothing was going to disturb or mess up my evening. Not even the reverend and his "discussions

# CHAPTER 15

## TY DOLLAR-SIGN

### Last Night

You're mothafuck'n right, I was about to get to the bottom of shit. Mothafuckas had the nerve to bring heat to my front door like it was sweet! Shit ain't never been sweet over here! Where da fuck they do that at?

I left Acorn and drove to Tiesha's spot on Myrtle. The bitch had the nerve to have an attitude about me banging on the door so late at night.

"Bitch! I'm not tryna hear none of that dumb shit right now—" I stormed past her, almost knocking her down.

"Bitch? Tyrone, I know yo punk ass didn't just barge up into my shit at dark thirty in the morning and call yourself calling me a bitch!" She cut me off.

I know Tiesha didn't play that "B" word, and I normally respect her enough never to call her a bitch. But a nigga was just dodging bullets like dodge balls. She was gonna have to respect my gangsta on this one.

"Look, fuck all that! A mothafucka just called themselves sliding through my trap and sending some mothafuck'n hot shit my way like that Bin Laden nigga. Now you and everybody else knows it's 'ABCG' on mine. Any-Body Can Get It."

"Which only tells me this had something to do with that fuck nigga that put his hands on you. Now since I don't know nothing about the fuck nigga, I suggest you go and put you on a pot of coffee or something and get to talking. I wanna know everything you know about the fuck nigga. Family, friends, kids, exes, the whole mothafuck'n taco. And I know you got

something to eat up in this joint. You might as well warm it up, cuz you know I'm hungry."

Considering that I wasn't a mothafucka who did too much explaining to nan mothafucka, Tiesha knew how serious I was. She didn't utter any other word until a plate of lasagna and garlic bread was steaming in front of me and a cup of coffee in front of her.

"Ty, Ugz has quite a few friends in Oakland and East Palo Alto. But he's one of them dudes that hangs around women, not niggaz." She stopped and took a sip from her coffee. I could tell she was holding back, but I decided not to press yet. After sipping from the coffee, she took a deep breath.

"Look, Ty, you don't even need to know all of that. He has a cousin over in the East named Phoenix. The two of them were thick as thieves. They were more like brothers than cousins. That fool had the nerve to call over here the other day with a bunch of drama, talking 'bout we gonna pay taking his folks from him—"

I cut her off ASAP! "And you didn't think I should've known about a mothafucka making threats about me?"

"Babe, these niggaz are the type to make a shit load of empty threats. I thought he was just venting and selling woof tickets, like the rest of these sorry ass niggaz." Tiesha is a hood bitch for real. Tough as nails. But she began to cry.

That shit fucked with the soft side of a nigga. I scooted my chair next to her and took her in a nigga'z arms.

"Ty, I didn't know the nigga would actually try and kill us."

She began to violently shake in my arms.

"It's okay, Tiesha, I got you, baby," I tried to reassure her.

"W-what if t-they c-come for me? Ty, I don't have shooters at my beck and call," she cried.

124

"Don't worry, I won't let anything happen to you." She was shaking so hard I was beginning to get nervous.

"Do you promise?" She took her head from my chest and looked me in my eyes.

"I promise," I told her before kissing her on the forehead.

The problem with bitches is they mean well, but they don't know shit. Because when niggaz be around them, all we show them is love and a bunch of other soft shit. They don't see the killer shit, so they be thinking all niggaz are all about them woof tickets. Until shit gets ugly.

I'm not some dumb bitch. I call shit how I see it and take it at face value. Whoever this nigga Phoenix was, he clearly wasn't no woof ticket. Not the way niggaz slid through my shit. That was some R.I.P. shit at its finest. Had the homie and I been some lesser niggaz, we might've been dead in this bitch.

It took a little over an hour and a half to calm Tiesha down and get her to go to sleep. The moment she was sleep, I was M.O.B.N., Mandatory On Them Bitch Niggaz.

I hit Jeff To Da Left on his cell about five times, but he didn't answer. Before I could hit the Twinz, Abel hit me. It would appear he learned the same shit that I learned. How, I don't know, but he was calling to fill me in.

I don't know why I hadn't heard his name before this. When we met up with the Twinz, Abel told me he knew all about Phoenix. The nigga was a few years older than us and was a big problem over in East Oakland.

That nigga was about to find out what that "Gas Nation" was about. The four of us rolled out to the East, to slide on one of Phoenix's top lieutenants. He has a spot over on 98th, half a block away from Brookfield. Supposedly, it was a cook spot.

We parked a few houses down the street from the spot and watched it for a while. All types of thoughts and images went through my mind.

"Let's go!" I told Kane, who sat patiently on the passenger side.

We crept up the street, blending in with the darkness. Abel fell in line behind us. From the front, the house only had two windows, which were both barred up. Thirty minutes later, Kane went and checked the back. One window. One set of bars. Each one of us had a five-gallon jug of gasoline in one hand, and our other hand gripped a cannon. But the main attraction was in our pockets.

"Y'all sure y'all got it?" I asked as we were crouched down on the side of the house, hiding in the shadows.

"It's all good," Abel answered. Kane just nodded his head.

"Alright, let's go!" I told them.

Kane and I moved towards the front of the house, while Abel crept around to the back. Immediately, Kane began to pour gasoline all over the front door, the porch and the dry grass in the front yard, covering about eight feet from the front door. By cutting off their escape route, whoever was in the house was about to burn alive fucking with me.

Thirty seconds later, we were watching the tiny flames lick at the blades of grass. Drinking up the gasoline, the flames grew, following the gasoline path up to the door. Within seconds, the entire front porch was ablaze.

Abel was in the backyard doing the same thing. Next, Kane and I grabbed bottles of Buzz Balls out of our pockets. They were filled with gasoline and made into cocktail bombs. One of the back windows broke. Followed by another. That was the sign that Kane and I had waited for. It was the sound of Kane sending his Buzz Balls through the back window.

I reached into my pocket for the first of four bottles. Once I lit it, I threw a fastball through the bars on the first window. Screams of panic were coming from inside the house. With the door opened, we could hear the cries and screams from within even clearer. There were both men and women trapped inside of the house, burning to death, paying for the sins of this nigga Phoenix.

"Dis Gas Nation, bitch!" I yelled out for any and all who just happened to be aware of what was going on to hear.

One nigga called out that the front porch was on fire. The heat from the flames was intensifying to the point where we were getting hot. We had to step back to the sidewalk.

Then the entire yard was ablaze. The night was illuminated by the flames, revealing all of the onlookers who'd formed on the streets.

Sirens could be heard in the distance. All of a sudden, a loud, ear-piercing noise was heard. It sounded like them old steam engine locomotives back in the day. This was our cue to get the fuck out of Dodge, something was about to blow.

"I'd surely hate to have been in that mothafucka. Blood, do you smell that shit?" Abel came walking up on my left-hand side.

"Fuck 'em. They know what time it was. If they didn't, somebody should've told them." I turned towards the two brothers. "Let's get the fuck outta here before that bitch blow."

"Oh fa'sho, it's gone blow. It's a meth lab. They got all kinds of industrial chemical bottles back there." Hearing Abel say this put a bit of pep in a nigga'z step.

No sooner when we reached the cars, the house blew. The blast was so mighty, it knocked down onlookers and blew out windows in cars. Even the ground shook. We rode all the way back to the Trap laughing, mocking the sounds of the niggaz trapped in the house.

Gas Nation, Bitch! Our presence fa'sho was known now.

## The Following Day

"Man, you already know that I was up as soon as the rooster pulled his cock out his bitch. I'm talking four-thirty-ish, five o'clock and that shit was on every channel. I'm talking Election Day coverage type shit." That was Jeff To Da Left going on about what we did to Phoenix's cook house last night.

"Nigga, I'm telling you the shit was like some Middle East, Bombs over Baghdad type shit. Yo, I'm telling you when that bitch blew up, I thought we were under siege," Abel called out before breaking out in a fit of laughter.

"You ole scary ass nigga. I swear to God, I thought Abel was going to stop, drop and roll right there on the sidewalk," I joked, teasing my little cousin.

We were all at the trap cutting dope and counting money. Talking shit and cracking jokes about last night.

"Shit nigga, I know you ain't over there talking! When that shit went up, Ty was shaking like he saw Jesus!" Abel shot back.

"P-pl-please, L-Lawd! I-I's didn't know he was one of yours. P-please fo'give me, Lawd!" Jeff To Da Left chimed in.

"Nigga, I know you ain't tryna clown, 'Mr. I missed the play because I was at twelve o'clock Sunday Mass'." I was on his ass for missing the play. Plus, he just made me mess up my count.

I put the stack down that was in my hands and started all over again from the first stack.

"Blood, I'm telling you, ole girl is a freak on a whole notha level. I'm talking some new generation sex games shit," Jeff To Da Left said.

"Nigga, fuck all of that! When are you finally gone tell us who it is?" I questioned. He's been spending more and more time with this mystery woman lately.

For the most part, a nigga'z personal life was his business. But this nigga was being so hush-hush! that it was beginning to not sit right. After all, mothafuckas couldn't have secrets in this game. Not in a family. Shit, secrets will kill a family.

Just then, Kane shocked everybody, especially me, when he spoke aloud what I was thinking.

"Secrets will kill a family and destroy an organization." Though he was looking at Jeff To Da Left, we all know he was talking to all of us.

"Nigga, y'all know I ain't got no secrets. Aaight, fuck it! We family. Y'all wanna know how deep this 'family' shit goes and exactly what shit means..."

"Nigga, speak on it!" I encouraged him.

"Nigga... nigga... Mama J.!" He spoke her name with finality, but I didn't catch it.

"Naaw, naaw playboy, don't bring her up now. I said, speak on it. We wanna know!" I chastised.

"Nigga, it's Mama J. I'm fucking Mama J." It took a minute for the shock of what he said to kick in on a nigga. I know he was pissed, but that wasn't no shit to joke about.

# CHAPTER 16

## JEFF TO DA LEFT

"Fuck outta here with the bullshit! You don't wanna expose the hoe, Nigga. She that important to you?" Ty Dollar-Sign was about to become irate; I could tell. I decided to defuse the situation.

"Nigga, you ain't listening. I'm serious, brah. I've been fucking Mama J. that's on Sittas." Sittas was a word we used when we were serious as fuck. It was like saying I put that on my Mama or Grams.

"Whoa! Whoa! Whoa! What the fuck you mean, you fucking Mama J?" The look on Abel's face was priceless. But the look on Ty's was even more extreme!

They wanted to know, so fuck it, I told them!

I started from the beginning and ran the whole thing down by them. I didn't have shit to hide. On the one hand, the shit that Mama J. and I were doing was wrong on so many levels. While on the other hand, I was being true and loyal to my brother and Mama J. by keeping my promise to them.

I swore I would be there for her by any means and I meant that shit. Nigga, that's what family is for. That's what family means. Loyalty to us and us alone. Besides it was a little too late to be wondering how niggaz were going to react to shit. We crossed a line that we couldn't uncross.

After running everything down to my brothers, I waited to see if any of them felt some kind of way or if they had anything to say on the matter, period.

"I'm not even 'bout to sit here and front. Now I don't mean no disrespect to either of you two, but I've seen the ass on her. Jeff To Da Left, nigga, I'll fuck the shit out of her too," Abel was the first one to speak up.

"You ain't never lied. For a little woman, Mama got hella shit back there." Those words leaving Dollar-Sign's mouth let me know there were no ill feelings or hard problems.

I checked the time on my phone. It was time for us to head to Richmond and meet up with Tasha's brother, Aubrey, to take care of our little artillery situation.

"Give me one second. Let me seal this last pack and it's good," Ty Dollar-Sign said.

We were getting money like crazy now. Our three trap spots were jumping like crazy. Now, I see why my nigga Jay wanted to be in the game. I wasn't even eighteen and I had a quarter of a million dollars stashed at Mama J's.

When Abel finished up, the four of us exited the back room of the trap. Scarface, Fat Boy and Hard-Work were in the front. Hard-Work is serving the fiends. Fat Boy has the Draco on his lap in case anything popped off. Scarface was overseeing the trap.

"Aaight, Face, we out this bitch." I gave him a one-hand gangsta hug.

"It's four of 'em back there for you." Abel let him know.

Fat Boy looked up only to make eye contact with Kane and give him a head nod. A silent conversation was had between two killah's and just like that, they both went back on point.

"Don't forget to call Meechie and tell him we are meeting up tonight," reminded Scarface.

"No doubt. I'm on it, rogue."

Scarface and Fat Boy were Norteños from MMN, Midtown Menlo Norteño. He made a little name for himself during the Summer of Blood a few years back as a shooter.

As one of the few remaining when Neva Die rose as the head of the reigns, his crew made a treaty with Neva Die and

Scarface was made a Black Lieutenant. When the situation with Ugz arose, Dollar-Sign reached out to Scarface for a favor. It was a lucrative favor that would pay off nicely. Not to mention, because of inner city beef, MMN didn't fuck with the blacks in East Palo Alto or Menlo Park who were in their twenties. Scarface knew Ugz was snitching, so in his mind, it was fuck Ugz and anybody who fucked with him.

Ty Dollar-Sign had full trust and respect in Scarface, enough to want him to oversee all three traps as our interim Trap Capo. So, we walked out of the trap with me being confident that I could focus solely on the meeting and our war with Phoenix.

It didn't take any time in the all-black Tahoe to make it to Central Richmond over by Warehouse District. Dollar-Sign drove while I was in the passenger seat. The Twinz were behind us on alert. All of us had baby Draco's on our laps. Tasha's brother, Aubrey, got shot yesterday and was in the hospital. Because we were already in the clutch, we had no choice but to fuck with his homeboy. A nigga named Booker.

When I ran Booker's license plates, the word came back that he was a stand-up, "Real Richmond" representative. I wasn't being too trusting though. Richmond niggaz were known goons, and some were grimy as fuck. Either way it went, I wasn't taking no losses which meant, "no chances."

Majority of the Warehouse District were out of business and abandoned. However, some were still fully operational. Luckily for us, all of them were closed by now.

We got to the meeting spot forty-five minutes early and when we pulled in, these mothafuckas was already there. See, that's that Richmond shit I'm talking about. We came early to get a feel for things. After all, we were meeting new niggaz on new turf. But this is these niggaz turf. What the fuck they so early for?

"I guess patna really believes the early bird gets the worm," Dollar-Sign said.

"Brah, if you think this nigga on some fuck shit, Left, just say the word and we'll start airing this bitch out now," Abel called from the back seat.

I thought for a moment. The shit didn't look right on the surface. But, if a nigga really looked at it, then dude could've just on his security shit.

"Naaw, it's good, lil brah. Let's see what's good. But I will tell you this here, if anything don't seem right, I'm talking a cricket or alley cat farts without our permission, then we gonna light this mothafucka up like the Chinese mothafuck'n New Year's." I was fa'sho about that.

We rolled to the back of the parking lot with everybody on edge. If the wind blew the wrong way, we were ready to go.

When we were about twenty feet away, we slowed to a stop. This was some real-life movie shit. Within seconds, three doors to the black Cadillac opened. Three, big, black ass niggaz stepped out. All of them looked like Somalian Mafia Refugees and all looked to be in their thirties.

"Alright, Twinz. Let's flex a little muscle," I told them.

"Say less," Abel responded, before grabbing the handle of the door and stepping out with his Draco in his hands. His brother did the same thing on the other side.

Had the Somalian looking mothafucka's not been holding AK-47's in their hands, I would not have flexed. Everyone stood still. The nigga on the passenger side, front door looked like he was summoning the Devil silently, begging him to make something pop off. The tension was visible. It was so thick!

"Come on, brah, before we all die out in this bitch tonight." I decided to step out of the truck so the supplier would know we had no ill intentions.

Ty Dollar-Sign followed me. Both of us made sure not to stand in either of the Twinz' lines of fire. The wind was relatively calm, considering the cold factor and the fact that we were standing on the docks.

Richmond sits right next to the Pacific Ocean. Which like San Francisco and a few other Bay Area cities, are actually slightly colder than all other Bay Area cities. This is because it sits so close to the water.

We stood there for at least two full minutes in the dark, cold of night, before there was a knock on the back-passenger window of the Escalade.

The scariest of the trio opened the door and I got the shock of a lifetime. I was expecting to see another Somalian pirate-looking mothafucka stepping out of the back. Boi, was I wrong!

The nigga was blacker than a mothafucka though, that Akon, Senegalese black. But the nigga was just that, a hundred and ten percent nigga. He was wearing an all-black and charcoal gray business suit that looked to be Prada, with some all-black Mauri alligators, and a pair of Tom Ford eyeglasses. All of this was on a five foot one or five foot two frame.

"Judging by the time of your arrival, one would assume you are either a very punctual individual who's slightly distrusting, or you're out to rob me. Going off of what I've heard about you, I will assume it's the earlier and not the latter. My only question for you would be, considering what your man's and 'em are holding in their hands, what is it that I can do for you?" he asked in a voice that could only be described as a high-pitched raspy voice.

"I need to supply an army with some shit that would get God's attention." I wasn't into beating around the bush.

"Armies are expensive, young man," he jabbed at me.

"So is my time."

"Oh, I see. So, I'll take it my original assessment about punctuality is correct. Well, in that case, allow me to get precisely to the point. I deal with high-end Ghost guns. If a gun is produced, I can Casper that mothafucka with no problem. But this mothafuck'n shit don't come cheap. I'm as punctual and detailed with my weapons as I am with my time. To me, early is on time and on time is too mothafuck'n late. You understand me?" He took his Tom Ford's off and tucked them inside of his vest, while whispering something to his bodyguard, who was so huge he made the arms dealer look like a midget in comparison.

The bodyguard pushed a button and the back of the Escalade opened.

"Allow me to show you something." Dollar-Sign and I followed Booker to the back of the Escalade. He walked like he was walking on pillows of clouds or some shit.

I couldn't help but to think that his charisma and his voice reminded me of the late singer, Prince.

"Now, these babies here are a personal favorite of mine." He reached into a green military arms crate. "The Ghost AR-15's. Now I have the normal AR-15's, as well as the Baby AR's. Both of these mothafuckas are accurate as fuck. Both the stock end and the barrel on the Baby AR are smaller and lighter and more compact. However, they both shoot 223's." He then picked up one of the AR pistols, which was around the size of a Desert Eagle.

"Now this little mothafucka shoots .223's with both accuracy and efficiency. As you can see, there are no identifying marks whatsoever on these babies. Not a serial

number, name, nothing besides the safety mechanism. I have thirty, fifty, and hundred-round clips for all. For the AR-15 and Baby AR, I also have one-hundred-fifty-round drums. All high velocity rounds." He tapped the trigger and a neon green infrared beam immediately appeared on the chest of one of the bodyguards.

"And what's the price tag on these lil babies?" I inquired.

I already knew what the AR-15's do. There was no question that when it came to choppas, the AR's were the elite. To have a mass abundance, fully untraceable, in a street war was the equivalent to having a black card in the fashion world.

"Are we talking for a group of homies or for an army?" he asked me with a smile in his eyes.

"I already told you I got an Army, O.G." Which I did.

While Dollar-Sign was building a trap cartel, I was drafting a small army of Gas Nation Soldiers.

"In that case, the AR-15's are normally fifteen hundred, I'll give them to you for seven hundred. The Baby AR's, let's do five hundred and for the pistols, five hundred, but you must buy at least ten." He sounded different now than he sounded when he was talking before. He was more business-like, more precise, like a math teacher.

"How many you got right now?"

He laughed a nasal laugh. "There's ten crates with fifteen in each crate. That's five guns apiece."

I turned towards Dollar-Sign. I didn't have to wonder what his decision was because it was written on his face. I looked back in Booker's direction.

"Booker, this is Ty Dollar-Sign, my right-hand, partner, and equal in the Gas Nation. He's also my brother. Judging by the look on his face, I'd say we'll take all ten of these crates

and will pay you ahead of time for ten more. Dollar-Sign, make it happen."

While Ty walked to the back of the Tahoe, Booker had a look on his face that said, "Y'all little mothafuckas better not try no funny shit."

Ty came back with two duffle bags. Each of the duffle bags carried a hundred thousand dollars. He placed the duffle bags on the ground by Booker and stepped back. The moment he did, all sorts of neon green lasers lit up the night. They were aimed at all four of us repp'n the Gas Nation.

"What the fuck?" Dollar-Sign called out. "O.G., you gonna rob us, my nigga?"

Booker paid him no attention. His head was cocked sideways, as if he was listening to something. That's when it hit me. Booker had lookouts posted and they picked up on De'Mario and CJ.

"You know something about a burgundy Astro van with two young brothas in it?" he asked me.

"Yeah, those are my little ones, De'Mario and CJ. I take it your lookouts spotted them before I could get a chance to tell you I had a van en route to pick up the crates."

He thought for a second. "Let them through," he spoke into a hidden microphone. "If it's as you say, we have a deal. If there is more to it than you say, then you little mothafuckas won't leave the parking lot. Real mothafuck'n Richmond!"

It was lucky for us that we didn't have anything up our sleeves. When De'Mario pulled up, two more Somalian mothfuckas appeared from nowhere and searched the van.

"Clear, Booker!" one of them called out, after searching the van from top to bottom.

The tension raised and everyone was happy as fuck. Especially me. Tasha would've kicked my ass if I would've

died out here in Richmond. I gave De'Mario the sign to get out of the van.

"God damn. Them niggaz swooped down on us in military vans and shit. Like they was military police and shit," C1ty said, as he climbed out of the van. His name was pronounced City, but he spelled it with a one in place of the letter *I*.

"You can never be too safe in the business. Mothafuckas are always trying to get over, or make you a vic. I refuse to ever be a victim," Booker told us.

"It's cool, O.G., because you definitely taught me a lesson tonight." And in truth, he did. Always expect the triple cross.

See, C1ty and CJ wasn't only here to pick up the crates. They were there as back-up. The van was equipped with a stash box that housed twin M-16's with six clips. Now I know that our back-up should always have back-up.

We completed the transaction and made arrangements to pick up the other fifteen cases. I could tell we'd just created a long-term business association.

# CHAPTER 17

## JEFF TO DA LEFT

Ordinarily, I wasn't the flashy type of nigga. However, Tasha's been begging me to take her shopping for almost two weeks and I just hadn't had time to do it. Today, I had no choice since I broke my Apple AirPods. I was going to the Hilltop Mall anyway to replace my AirPods. So, I decided today after church was going to be a good day to tear down the mall.

It seemed like Mama J. had an attitude when I told her that Tasha and I was going to spend the day shopping. I don't know if it was out of jealousy or what, but I figure she will get over it. I'm sure a nice gift for herself would help the cause.

Tasha and I stopped by Acorns first, so I could pick up two Louis bags. Yeah, it was time to get my mothafuck'n shine on. To ensure I was on mack mode, I decided we would take the new Lexus truck I'd bought her as a "just because" gift a couple of weeks ago. The truck was champagne pink, with twenty-four-inch Ashanti's. All chrome, to shine like my baby.

We started at Saks Fifth Avenue, where I dropped twelve stacks on Balmain outfits for me, and ten stacks on a gang of high-end shit for her. Everything from Prada to Fendi. We had a ball.

An hour or so later, a nigga had so many bags in our hands that we had to walk out and drop them off in the truck before we went on our second run. This also gave me the opportunity to grab the second Louis bag from C1ty and CJ, who were on a low-key scrimmage, ducked off in the parking lot parked two cars away.

They trailed Tasha and me around the mall incognito, just in case there were niggaz lurking and they thought shit was sweet. Since I learned my lesson about backing up the back-up plan, there were also two more nondescriptive cars with Gas Nation hittas parked in the parking lot. Everybody was armed with the Ghost AR-15's and Baby AR's just in case something went down.

I made sure to spoil my baby. Partly because she deserved it and partly because I felt guilty about fucking Mama J. On the way out the mall, I found a place to replace my AirPods. I was checking out the latest designs when the service girl asked me, "Uh, excuse me, aren't you Jeffrey Watkins?" She was a bad-ass black and white mixed bitch.

"I mean, damn ma, you all out here broadcasting a nigga'z government like you're the IRS collector." Tasha was standing right by my side, so ain't like a nigga was out of pocket or anything.

"I don't think you know me." She blushed and put her hand over her mouth.

"Well, okay of course you don't know me. My name is Natalia. I go to Castlemont High School and I believe I have what you are looking for." God damn, this little light-skinned, mixed bitch was bold.

She was bad than a mothafucka with hair that went down to her ass. Her eyes and accent told me that she was mixed with something, even if her skin tone didn't. Sounded Yugoslavian or some shit.

"Oh, excuse me, bitch. Don't think because you got those pretty ass blue eyes and that expensive ass weave that shit is sweet over here. Bitch, I will fuck you up and mop the floor with you in this mothafuck'n store." Although she spoke with venom, Tasha didn't yell or cause a scene.

"No, it's not like that. I wouldn't disrespect you like that, sistah, and I don't want yo man. Believe me I don't. This is in regard to his late brother Jay. I have some information... I think... No, I know, you will want to hear!"

Jay's name was the absolute last thing I expected to hear come out of her mouth. I'm not going to lie. It threw me off. Naw, it fucked me up!

"What you mean, information about Jay?" I took a step towards her. Subconsciously not thinking nor paying attention to the gesture.

"Look, I can't talk here, my supervisor is a complete ass and this internship is for college credits. I don't need the money. I need the credits. Take my number down and call me. I get off in a couple of hours and we can talk then. I think we can help each other," she told me, just as a big Russian-looking mothafucka approached us.

"Is everything okay, Natalia?"

"I hope for your sake, everything is okay. I'd hate to see you get aired the fuck out up in this bitch," C1ty spoke as he came up from behind the Russian.

"Kevin, it's okay," she told him and then continued to speak to him in some weird language. I don't know what she told him, but he backed the fuck up and disappeared back to wherever the fuck he came from.

"Excuse Kevin, he is one of my bodyguards and very overprotective of me. As I was saying, please take down my number and call me. I know what happened to Jay." How could a nigga refuse something like that?

If this little bitch knew something about Jay's death on Gas Nation, I needed to hear this shit out. I put her number in my phone and told her I would call as soon as she got off work. Then I thought about it and gave her my number for her to call me the moment she clocked off work.

Tasha and I then left the mall with about ten more bags and I drove her home. Before the run-in with Natalia, I may have tried to get some because she and I hadn't done anything about a possible lead to Jay's murder.

We walked the entire ride back about it and what a nigga would do if it was true. Finally, after talking for about an hour or so. I helped her carry all of her bags upstairs.

Mama J. seemed to be in a better mood when I walked through the door. The apartment smelled like Down South Sunday evening. I'm talking that Big Mama in the kitchen all day Sunday: Louisiana, Mississippi, Arkansas, Georgia style cooking.

Her back was towards me as she stood over the stove. Damn, Mama J. had a nice ass. It was perfectly round and huge as fuck. I walked up her and wrapped my arms around her and kissed her on the back of her neck.

"Boy, don't you come all up in here kissing on me without washing yourself off after kissing on and only God knows what else with that little girl." She feigned pulling away from me, but it was a halfhearted try.

"See, now that's where you went wrong, all we did was go shopping." I wanted to tell her about Natalia and the possibility of the information she claimed to have had. I didn't want to jump the gun in case it was a bunch of bullshit.

"So, why are you all in here on me, instead of with your little girlfriend? I'm sure she would still enjoy your company."

I turned her around by her shoulders so that she could focus on me. "So, you trying to tell me you don't enjoy my company any longer?" Before she could answer, I began kissing softly on her neck, but she didn't go anywhere.

"Don't worry. I'm not trying to start anything. I have some important business I got to take care of tonight. I just wanted

to give you this before I got ready." I pulled out a Tiffany's bag and handed it to her.

Inside were three boxes. They contained a matching necklace and earrings. When she saw the jewelry, she was every bit excited. After passionately kissing me, she promised that she would thank me appropriately later when I got back.

**\*\*\* 3X \*\*\***

# CHAPTER 18

## TY DOLLAR-SIGN

I didn't trust the bitch Natalia not one bit. When Jeff To Da Left called me and told me what happened, I immediately was skeptical.

When I ran her license plates, or did a background check on her, no one knew who she was. Which only added to my doubt and raised my suspicions, making me more skeptical.

Fuck it! I brought the Nation out. We were eight vehicles deep, with two hittas in each vehicle. Four of the vehicles were hidden, yet the main body of four drove right up to the all-you-can-eat diner.

The Twinz were given a green light, trained to go at the first sign of fuckery.

The eight of us entered the restaurant, while the other eight took up positions outside. Besides Natalia's people, only a few people were in the diner. Judging by their looks, they were the "mind their business" types.

Jeff To Da Left led the way to the back of the diner where she sat, with four bodyguards of her own.

"I heard you guys didn't play games." She was hinting at our numbers. "But I wasn't expecting these guys. Have a seat please." She gestured towards the empty seats across from her.

"The Gas Nation moves mean when we need to," Jeff To Da Left told her as he took the seat and scooted in the booth.

"You know it's funny you say that because when I ran your license plate, I came up blank." I told her.

She simply smiled before saying. "You just didn't look deep or enough. You see, on the surface I am just an ordinary person, a child getting ready for college. I am much deeper than that. I am getting ready to take over one of the world's

largest drug operations." She paused to see the effect those words had on us.

"It was Jeff To Da Left that spoke. "So tell me, with connections like that, what could you possibly want with us?"

"More connections. Everyone believes money buys power. I believe money simply produces ways to become powerful. But it is through your connections that you actually become powerful. With ten G's on your head, I could probably have you hit. However, with ten organizations throughout the West Coast, I most assuredly will have you killed. See, so it's your connections that make you powerful. Who you know and how well you know them determines what they can and will do for you or because of you."

"I have it in good faith that you guys have been eagerly looking for the person or persons responsible for killing Jay." She gestured to one of her bodyguards, who sat on an iPad on the table and brought the screen up.

"There is an old hangar by the old Army base. Inside of this hangar is the man responsible for killing Jay. He has an interesting story to tell, should you be interested in listening. However, whether you choose to do so or not, I am prepared to give you or take you to his location, in turn for you guys to take care of something for me."

I was really fucked up! Who the fuck was this bitch? Before anyone could react, I upped both of my Glock 40's that were on my waist and had them pointed in her pretty little face. These bitches stayed cocked and loaded.

"Look, bitch. I don't know who you are, why you're here or what the fuck you came for. But I should blow your cock-sucking head off for playing with us. Bringing us the fuck out here for nothing. If the hood don't know who killed my brother, then how in the fuck yo pretty little pale ass gone know? Now bitch, you got five seconds to tell us what you

want before I part yo shit like Red Sea!" I was furious. Bitch tryna play me and my niggaz. I'll blow her shit back to Russia!

To my surprise, none of her bodyguards moved an inch. Nor did she seem worried. Maybe it's because I didn't see the five red dots all congressing on the center of my chest.

"I would like for you to lower your guns before my man gets nervous and replaces those dots on your chest with blood." It was then that I saw the dots. "I assure you I don't play, and this isn't a game. I'm sure you know the name, Bernard Johnson. Look into the iPad," she told Jeff To Da Left.

He reached for the iPad and grabbed it off of the table. "Dollar-Sign, put 'em away," was all he said. He put the pad down and looked the bitch dead in her eyes. "This favor you want from us, what exactly is it?"

"I want you to kill some of the people that may stand in my way to getting what's rightfully mine."

"How many are we talking about?" C1ty asked.

She smiled. "A few."

"To get answers about Jay, it doesn't matter. I'd kill a thousand," Jeff To Da Left said.

*** 3X ***

## JEFF TO DA LEFT

The old Army base was right in the Port of Oakland, which made the old hangar Bernard was being held in, very cold and damp. It was so dark inside, makeshift battery-operated lamps were hung up to provide light to the medium-sized storage hangar.

I could tell the hangar had been nonoperational for quite some time. It reeked of old mildew and built-up dust. The only

thing in the room was a metal chair that was bolted to the ground.

"W-who's there? Who's there, God dammit?" Bernard called out from the hangar. He was stripped butt naked and tied to the chair. I didn't know if he was shivering from the cold or from fear, or both. I walked up to him and tore off the blindfold that concealed his eyes. When they adjusted and he saw me, he became puzzled.

"J-Jeff-Jeffery, what are you doing here? What am I doing here?"

"I was going to ask you the same question, Deacon." Not only was Bernard one of the head deacons at church, he was also Jay's uncle.

I had both fire and venom ready to spew forth from me. I didn't know what Jay's uncle had to do with this, but I was going to find out.

"J-Jeff, look young brotha, I don't know. I was kidnapped leaving Bible Study the other night. I don't know what's going on," he cried.

"Uncle Bernard. Who killed Jay?"

"W-what. W-hat do you m-mean, who killed Jay? Come on, nephew, how would I know that?" I could see the look change on his face and the sound of his voice change.

Uncle Bernard was lying.

"Excuse me, Mr. Watkins, but if you allow me," Natalia broke in.

"What?"

She spoke to one of her guards. Moments later, the door to the hangar opened up and two more of her men brought in Uncle Bernard's wife and three daughters.

"Mr. O'Henry, my name is Natalia. I don't mind telling you this because you are a dead man."

"Daddy!" one of the girls called out upon hearing his name. Although all four of the females were blindfolded, they were not gagged.

"I-It's okay, Chanelle, it's okay…" He told his second to the oldest daughter.

"Bernard! Lord Jesus. Baby, what is going on?" his wife Beverly asked him.

"It's all going to be alright, Beverly. Just be strong."

"I am sorry, Beverly, but that isn't true. Nikoli, remove her blindfold," Natalia said.

"Who are you?"

"Mrs. O'Henry, I'm sorry but I don't play games. It seems however, that your husband does. Say bye to your husband," Natalia told her.

"W-wait a minute, what?"

*Psst*! Without hesitation, Natalia pulled out a 9mm with a silencer on it from inside her jacket, and shot Mrs. O'Henry in the middle of her forehead at point-blank range. Her blood and brains added a coppery smell to the mildew and dust in the room.

Bernard went crazy!

God damn! I didn't think little mama had that in her, but seeing how she got down made me turn up!

The daughters were screaming and hollering. Four good knocks upside their father's head with my Glock shut them up.

"Every time I ask you a question and you lie, I will kill one of your daughters," Natalia told him.

"Mom?" The oldest daughter put two and two together after hearing something hit the floor and the sound of the silenced gun.

"I'm sorry, Stephanie dear, but your mom is dead. Maybe you should tell your daddy to cooperate, so you and your sisters don't die next." Natalia's voice was ice cold.

"Okay! Okay! Just don't hurt my girls. I'll tell you what you want to know!" he shouted.

"Who killed Jay?" I asked him.

"I did!"

I was not expecting him to say that.

*BOCCA*! I shot him in his left leg.

Once he calmed back down, I asked Deacon Bernard O'Henry, the million-dollar question. "Why?"

"Sister Johnson! She blackmailed me into doing it..."

*BOCCA*! *BOCCA*!

There went his right knee and his stomach.

"You son of a bitch, don't lie to me!"

He howled in pain. Even his girls cried, screamed and yelled. I didn't give a fuck.

How could he say this about Mama J.? I was about to shoot him again, until Dollar-Sign reached out and grabbed my arm.

I lowered my arm. "Get them girls out of here."

Natalia had her men follow my order.

After waiting for the girls to leave, I forced Bernard to tell me what the fuck was going on. He told me a tale I was not ready for. One of rape, murder, jealousy and blackmail.

Thirty gruesome minutes later, I felt like I needed to go to confession, just from the shit I heard.

Together, Dollar-Sign and I stood shoulder to shoulder and filled Deacon O'Henry with sixty slugs for killing our brother. This shit wasn't a game. Revenge Is Promised!

The arrangement we worked out with Natalia was that we would tend to some of our pressing matters and then carry out her request. She wanted to know what to do with O'Henry's daughters. They hadn't seen our faces nor heard anything incriminating and I wasn't with killing kids. We tied them up and left them somewhere, where they would be found in the morning.

3X Krazy

*** 3X ***

# CHAPTER 19

## JEFF TO DA LEFT

I couldn't believe what I heard at all. Mama J. could not have had Jay murdered. Not her own son. Not my brother.

The more and more I thought about it, the more and more I was beginning to see some truth in his story.

*"Blow out yo mothafucking brains/hit'em, get'em, up kill'em all up like Norman Bates got me going insane /Darfar!"*

A double bottle of Rémy Martin and 3X Krazy blasting through my speakers is how I was dealing with it.

Tasha sat in the passenger seat with a pair of earbuds, listening to the entire incident with Deacon O'Henry, our beloved Uncle Bernard. I had recorded the entire thing on my phone since she was unable to be there with us in person.

It was a little after 9:00 p.m. the following night. I'd spent all day listening to music and drinking the pain away. Now it was time to honor our promises to each other and to my brother Jay. It was time to ultimately show our loyalty.

I took another swing out of the bottle and passed it back to Dollar-Sign. I reached into the ashtray and grabbed a blunt. I lit it while listening to Keak da Sneak spit his verse.

*"/... Dopefiend said keep running little dude I think they on you/ fuck it! / Hit him across the head with the heater cause if I don't get away you ain't leaving this bitch either.... /"*

*"/ The Dome Cracker, The Wig Splitta, The Grave Digger/ All about my cheddar square ass nigga/ Hat'n on a playa Cause I'm all about my fast cars guns gone gitcha, gitcha when I hit cha block. It's gone feel like a gorilla. /*

That's what we were. The Dome Cracker, The Wig Splitta, and The Grave Digger. We were just waiting on the reaper.

When Tasha was finally done listening to the entire recording, she took the earbuds out of her ears and shook her head in silence. I didn't wait for her to speak. When she took the blunt I held out for her, I stepped out of my truck.

A thousand and one thoughts swarmed through my mind as I made my way inside the building. I don't know which was heavier, my heart or my feet as I climbed the stars.

It seemed like I took forever to finally reach the door. When I did, I let myself in.

Betty Wright's "Tonight is The Night" was playing on the speakers when I closed the door. Mama J. was in the living room watching television.

"I see you finally decided to make it home," she told me as I made my way across the room.

"We have to talk." The sound of my voice took her focus off of the screen and she looked my way.

"Baby, what's wrong?"

"Turn that off." She complied with my demand.

"That important business I had last night was tracking down Jay's murderer." I watched her breath get caught inside her chest.

"Did you find him?" Her voice trembled.

"He's dead."

She didn't say anything for a while after I told her this. Her nightgown rose and fell as her breathing increased. I stood silently. Waiting.

Finally, she spoke. "D-did he tell you anything?" I could hear the fear as she asked the question.

*** **3X** ***

## Last Night

*"What the fuck you mean, Mama J. blackmailed you to kill her son? Nigga, that shit you talking don't fly!" Looking at Uncle Bernard, all I had was murder in my heart. But I had to get to the bottom, or else my mind and soul wouldn't rest.*

*"She told me she could no longer live with the pain or the shame of the lie she had been living all of these years, from what we did to her—"*

*"What. Who's us?" I cut him off*

*"Me and my brother."*

*I thought your brother ran off when Jay was born?" I was really confused now.*

*"Reverend Jacobs is my brother."*

*"What?"*

*"He's my oldest brother. Ever since we were kids, Robert has had issues. Sexual issues regarding younger girls and boys. I'll just call it a sickness and a disease. As we got older, his sickness not only progressed but somehow, he managed to get me involved. Though reluctantly, I might add. But nevertheless, I became involved with his behind the door sessions. Or his 'Open-door Policy,' as he called it. Before long, the sessions became a weekly thing. A weekend of debauchery in the worst sexual way possible. It began with the forced sexual assault on Sistah Johnson, who said she refused to partake in the molestation any longer. Her and three other girls were victimized by us and months later, three of the four became pregnant. Of course, they were all impregnated by my brother. We were sure of this because I am sterile. My children were sperm donor conceptions—"*

*"So, you mean to tell me you two sick fucks have been raping and molesting children in the church house!" I interrupted.*

157

*"I'm sorry to say, but yes!" He spoke as if he'd become drained, like a man getting ready for state execution, who'd been given his last rights.*

I didn't even bother telling her everything Uncle Bernard confessed to me. There was no need. Her tearstained face was proof enough that Bernard's bitch ass was telling somewhat of the truth. At least enough to trigger a nerve inside of Mama J.

"You don't understand," she cried.

Just then, there was a knock at the door. I left her reliving her nightmares and secrets, right there on the couch and went to answer the door.

Dollar-Sign and Tasha came walking into the apartment. It was only right that we all get to the bottom of this, since we all made a pact. After all, we were all a part of it. In it together and linked beyond belief. Now more than ever.

The three of us made our way into the living room. Upon seeing us, Mama J. began crying even harder. "But you don't understand! You don't understand! They raped us repeatedly over and over. They took our youth and our innocence. Oh, Dear Lord, help these children understand."

"What did that have to do with our brother?" I asked. It's as if a piece of the puzzle was still missing.

"He was your real brother," she mumbled under her breath.

"W-what? What you say?" I know I didn't hear what I thought I just heard.

Mama J. took a moment to gather her composure before she spoke again. "I said Javari was your real brother and Tasha is your sister. All of us mothers, were the girls those Devils raped and molested. We all got pregnant together. The church threatened and blackmailed our parents and families into

158

coming up with cover-up stories to protect the church and its evil sins." The tears flowed from her eyes down her face.

"Bitch! Are you telling me all of you sat by and didn't say shit as I fucked and was going to marry my own sister? What kind of sick twisted shit is that?" I was seeing red.

"Baby, please don't speak to me like that. Jeffrey, I love you. You can't marry Tasha since she's your sister. But we can be together. You and I—"

"Bitch, have you lost your rabbit-ass mind?" Tasha jumped on top of Mama J. whaling away, blow after blow.

Dollar-Sign and I let Tasha get some of her anger off of her chest before we pulled her off of Mama J.

I really didn't need to ask her why she did it. Uncle Bernard already told us that Mama J. thought God was punishing her by allowing her to get pregnant by her rapist. When Javari was born, she thought God forgave her and replaced her pain with a blessing. The love of a child.

When Jay chose the streets over the church, it dug up all of Mama J.'s hurt and pain, making her remember and relive every painful memory of the details. She told him she felt as if the Devil was taunting her, day in and day out. It drove her crazy. When she finally couldn't take it any longer, she blackmailed Bernard into killing his real blood nephew.

"You are a poor excuse for a woman, and you were an even worse mother. I'm sorry for what them niggaz did to you, but I promise you they won't get away with it. They will be following you." The time for talking was over. We didn't come to talk. We came for Revenge, because Revenge Is Promised. The three of us pulled out our Glock 40's.

"Revenge is promised, anybody can get it!" the three of us quoted.

*BOCCA! BOCCA! BOCCA! BOCCA! BOCCA!*
*BOCCA! BOCCA! BOCCA! BOCCA! BOCCA!*

Mama J.'s body jumped and jerked as the bullets crashed into her body, bringing about justice.

When we were done carrying out our revenge, I grabbed my duffle bags of money and the three of us walked out of the apartment, getting ready to see how we will deal with the cards life just dealt us. See how they played.

*** **3X** ***

# CHAPTER 20

## TASHA

I exited my Lexus truck on the dark stormy night with my mind made up. My intentions weren't necessarily clear, but my actions would be.

I was wearing six-inch, all-black stilettos to match the all-black, floor-length, leather trench coat I had on. Underneath, I was bare as the day I was born. I was on a mission today to do the Devil's work.

I had been sitting parked outside the church for twenty-odd minutes, getting ready to face the truth.

Now was the time! I entered the church through the side door in the back. It was a door I'd used many times before. It was the door that led directly to the corridor leading to the reverend's private chamber.

Like I knew he would be, Reverend Jacobs was sitting at his desk awaiting my arrival. When he saw me, a sparkle ignited in his eyes. My guess, it was from the anticipation of what we were going to do. What we have always done.

"Aah yes, my lovely Angel, Tasha. How are you doing this beautiful evening that the Lord Our Father has blessed us with?" he asked me in the sincerest voice he could muster up. The fucking monster!

"I'm fine, Daddy, now that I'm here with you." He's been having me call him Daddy for years now, while doing his sick, twisted, sexual exploits. Ever since he stole my innocence. However, calling him that now felt twice as hard.

As I walked over behind his desk, he scooted his chair backwards, making room for me on his lap. This was our normal routine.

I couldn't believe this was my father. This was the man who was supposed to love and protect me from the many evils of the world. Instead, he was one of the world's demons, preying on my purity. Draining me of my essence. For years, he's been molesting me and threatening me. I didn't realize at the time what he really was doing was brainwashing me, while he had sex with me.

"I have something I need to tell you," I whispered into his ear as I licked his earlobe.

His strong, rough hands were already greedily roaming under my coat. Rubbing across my body.

"What is it, Angel?" he asked me.

"I'm pregnant." I could feel his body tense up underneath me. "Isn't that wonderful news? Now we'll have proof of our love."

I was no fool. There was no love. Only proof of a grave injustice, a major infraction invaded upon my privacy. But no more.

As I kissed down to his neck, I made my way to the other side of his head and kissed his other ear. His dry hand was cupping and squeezing on my ass cheek, while the other fondled my breast.

I couldn't take it any longer, my skin crawled like a thousand centipedes were under its surface.

It had to end now.

*Now or Never*! I slid the razor blade from under my tongue, the cold steel matching the ice in my veins.

"Revenge Is Promised, Daddy!" I whispered.

In one swift motion, I clenched the blade in my teeth and slid it across his monstrous throat. The blood gushed out as the blade slid across his carotid artery. His eyes got big. His grip on my ass was vise-like until the life oozed out of his body.

"Bye, Daddy." I made my way back out the same way that I came in.

Once I was back out in the night, the rain was pouring down heavily. I took my coat off and stood in the nude with my head tilted back as the rain washed away all traces of blood off my impregnated body.

Minutes later I was in my truck, driving off wondering how I was going to tell Jeff, *my brother*, I was pregnant with my daddy's baby.

*Our brother*!

**To Be Continued...**
**3X Krazy 2**
**Coming Soon**

# Submission Guideline

Submit the first three chapters of your completed manuscript to ldpsubmissions@gmail.com, subject line: Your book's title. The manuscript must be in a .doc file and sent as an attachment. Document should be in Times New Roman, double spaced and in size 12 font. Also, provide your synopsis and full contact information. If sending multiple submissions, they must each be in a separate email.

Have a story but no way to send it electronically? You can still submit to LDP/Ca$h Presents. Send in the first three chapters, written or typed, of your completed manuscript to:

**LDP: Submissions Dept**
**Po Box 944**
**Stockbridge, Ga 30281**

*DO NOT send original manuscript. Must be a duplicate.*

Provide your synopsis and a cover letter containing your full contact information.

Thanks for considering LDP and Ca$h Presents.

**<u>Coming Soon from Lock Down Publications/Ca$h Presents</u>**

BOW DOWN TO MY GANGSTA

By **Ca$h**

TORN BETWEEN TWO

By **Coffee**

THE STREETS STAINED MY SOUL **II**

By **Marcellus Allen**

BLOOD OF A BOSS **VI**

SHADOWS OF THE GAME II

By **Askari**

LOYAL TO THE GAME **IV**

By **T.J. & Jelissa**

IF LOVING YOU IS WRONG... **III**

By **Jelissa**

TRUE SAVAGE **VII**

MIDNIGHT CARTEL III

DOPE BOY MAGIC IV

CITY OF KINGZ II

By **Chris Green**

BLAST FOR ME **III**

A SAVAGE DOPEBOY III

CUTTHROAT MAFIA III

By **Ghost**

A HUSTLER'S DECEIT III

KILL ZONE **II**

BAE BELONGS TO ME III

De'Kari

A DOPE BOY'S QUEEN III

By **Aryanna**

COKE KINGS V

KING OF THE TRAP II

By **T.J. Edwards**

GORILLAZ IN THE BAY V

3X KRAZY II

**De'Kari**

THE STREETS ARE CALLING II

**Duquie Wilson**

KINGPIN KILLAZ IV

STREET KINGS III

PAID IN BLOOD III

CARTEL KILLAZ IV

DOPE GODS III

**Hood Rich**

SINS OF A HUSTLA II

**ASAD**

KINGZ OF THE GAME VI

**Playa Ray**

SLAUGHTER GANG IV

RUTHLESS HEART IV

By **Willie Slaughter**

THE HEART OF A SAVAGE III

By **Jibril Williams**

FUK SHYT II

By **Blakk Diamond**

166

THE REALEST KILLAZ III

**By Tranay Adams**

TRAP GOD III

**By Troublesome**

YAYO IV

GHOST MOB

**Stilloan Robinson**

KINGPIN DREAMS III

**By Paper Boi Rari**

CREAM II

**By Yolanda Moore**

SON OF A DOPE FIEND III

**By Renta**

FOREVER GANGSTA II

GLOCKS ON SATIN SHEETS III

**By Adrian Dulan**

LOYALTY AIN'T PROMISED III

**By Keith Williams**

THE PRICE YOU PAY FOR LOVE II

**By Destiny Skai**

CONFESSIONS OF A GANGSTA II

**By Nicholas Lock**

I'M NOTHING WITHOUT HIS LOVE II

SINS OF A THUG II

**By Monet Dragun**

LIFE OF A SAVAGE IV

A GANGSTA'S QUR'AN III

MURDA SEASON III

GANGLAND CARTEL II

By **Romell Tukes**

QUIET MONEY III

THUG LIFE II

By **Trai'Quan**

THE STREETS MADE ME III

By **Larry D. Wright**

THE ULTIMATE SACRIFICE VI

IF YOU CROSS ME ONCE II

ANGEL III

By **Anthony Fields**

FRIEND OR FOE III

By **Mimi**

SAVAGE STORMS II

By **Meesha**

BLOOD ON THE MONEY II

**By J-Blunt**

THE STREETS WILL NEVER CLOSE II

**By K'ajji**

NIGHTMARES OF A HUSTLA II

**By King Dream**

THE WIFEY I USED TO BE II

**By Nicole Goosby**

## **Available Now**

RESTRAINING ORDER **I & II**

By **CA$H & Coffee**

LOVE KNOWS NO BOUNDARIES **I II & III**

By **Coffee**

RAISED AS A GOON I, II,  III & IV

BRED BY THE SLUMS I, II, III

BLAST FOR ME I & II

ROTTEN TO THE CORE I II III

A BRONX TALE I, II, III

DUFFEL BAG CARTEL I II III IV

HEARTLESS GOON I II III IV

A SAVAGE DOPEBOY I II

HEARTLESS GOON I II III

DRUG LORDS I II III

CUTTHROAT MAFIA I II

By **Ghost**

LAY IT DOWN **I & II**

LAST OF A DYING BREED

BLOOD STAINS OF A SHOTTA I & II III

By **Jamaica**

LOYAL TO THE GAME I II III

LIFE OF SIN I, II III

By **TJ & Jelissa**

BLOODY COMMAS I & II

SKI MASK CARTEL I  II & III

KING OF NEW YORK I II,III IV V

RISE TO POWER I II III

COKE KINGS I II III IV

BORN HEARTLESS I II III IV

KING OF THE TRAP

By **T.J. Edwards**

IF LOVING HIM IS WRONG…I & II

LOVE ME EVEN WHEN IT HURTS I II III

By **Jelissa**

WHEN THE STREETS CLAP BACK I & II III

THE HEART OF A SAVAGE I II

By **Jibril Williams**

A DISTINGUISHED THUG STOLE MY HEART I II & III

LOVE SHOULDN'T HURT I II III IV

RENEGADE BOYS I II III IV

PAID IN KARMA I II III

SAVAGE STORMS

By **Meesha**

A GANGSTER'S CODE I &, II III

A GANGSTER'S SYN I II III

THE SAVAGE LIFE I II III

CHAINED TO THE STREETS I II III

BLOOD ON THE MONEY

By **J-Blunt**

PUSH IT TO THE LIMIT

By **Bre' Hayes**

BLOOD OF A BOSS **I, II, III, IV, V**

SHADOWS OF THE GAME

By **Askari**

THE STREETS BLEED MURDER **I, II & III**

THE HEART OF A GANGSTA I II& III

By **Jerry Jackson**

CUM FOR ME I II III IV V VI

An **LDP Erotica Collaboration**

BRIDE OF A HUSTLA **I  II & II**

THE FETTI GIRLS **I, II& III**

CORRUPTED BY A GANGSTA I, II III, IV

BLINDED BY HIS LOVE

THE PRICE YOU PAY FOR LOVE

DOPE GIRL MAGIC I II III

By **Destiny Skai**

WHEN A GOOD GIRL GOES BAD

By **Adrienne**

THE COST OF LOYALTY I II III

**By Kweli**

A GANGSTER'S REVENGE **I II III & IV**

THE BOSS MAN'S DAUGHTERS I II III IV V

A SAVAGE LOVE  **I & II**

BAE BELONGS TO ME I II

A HUSTLER'S DECEIT I, II, III

WHAT BAD BITCHES DO I, II, III

SOUL OF A MONSTER I II III

KILL ZONE

A DOPE BOY'S QUEEN I II

By **Aryanna**

A KINGPIN'S AMBITON

A KINGPIN'S AMBITION **II**

I MURDER FOR THE DOUGH

By **Ambitious**

TRUE SAVAGE I II III IV V VI

DOPE BOY MAGIC I, II, III

MIDNIGHT CARTEL I II

CITY OF KINGZ

By **Chris Green**

A DOPEBOY'S PRAYER

By **Eddie "Wolf" Lee**

THE KING CARTEL **I, II & III**

By **Frank Gresham**

THESE NIGGAS AIN'T LOYAL **I, II & III**

By **Nikki Tee**

GANGSTA SHYT **I II &III**

By **CATO**

THE ULTIMATE BETRAYAL

By **Phoenix**

BOSS'N UP **I , II & III**

By **Royal Nicole**

I LOVE YOU TO DEATH

**By Destiny J**

I RIDE FOR MY HITTA

I STILL RIDE FOR MY HITTA

By **Misty Holt**

LOVE & CHASIN' PAPER

By **Qay Crockett**

TO DIE IN VAIN

SINS OF A HUSTLA

By **ASAD**

BROOKLYN HUSTLAZ

By **Boogsy Morina**

BROOKLYN ON LOCK I & II

By **Sonovia**

GANGSTA CITY

By **Teddy Duke**

A DRUG KING AND HIS DIAMOND I & II III

A DOPEMAN'S RICHES

HER MAN, MINE'S TOO I, II

CASH MONEY HO'S

THE WIFEY I USED TO BE

By **Nicole Goosby**

TRAPHOUSE KING **I II & III**

KINGPIN KILLAZ I II III

STREET KINGS I II

PAID IN BLOOD **I II**

CARTEL KILLAZ I II III

DOPE GODS I II

By **Hood Rich**

LIPSTICK KILLAH **I, II, III**

CRIME OF PASSION I II & III

FRIEND OR FOE I II

By **Mimi**

STEADY MOBBN' **I, II, III**

THE STREETS STAINED MY SOUL

By **Marcellus Allen**

WHO SHOT YA **I, II, III**

SON OF A DOPE FIEND I II

**Renta**

GORILLAZ IN THE BAY **I II III IV**

TEARS OF A GANGSTA I II

3X KRAZY

**DE'KARI**

TRIGGADALE I II III

**Elijah R. Freeman**

GOD BLESS THE TRAPPERS I, II, III

THESE SCANDALOUS STREETS I, II, III

FEAR MY GANGSTA I, II, III IV, V

THESE STREETS DON'T LOVE NOBODY I, II

BURY ME A G I, II, III, IV, V

A GANGSTA'S EMPIRE I, II, III, IV

THE DOPEMAN'S BODYGAURD I II

THE REALEST KILLAZ I II

**Tranay Adams**

THE STREETS ARE CALLING

**Duquie Wilson**

MARRIED TO A BOSS… I II III

**By Destiny Skai & Chris Green**

KINGZ OF THE GAME I II III IV V

**Playa Ray**
SLAUGHTER GANG I II III
RUTHLESS HEART I II III
**By Willie Slaughter**
FUK SHYT
**By Blakk Diamond**
DON'T F#CK WITH MY HEART I II
**By Linnea**
ADDICTED TO THE DRAMA I II III
**By Jamila**
YAYO I II III
A SHOOTER'S AMBITION I II
**By S. Allen**
TRAP GOD  I II
**By Troublesome**
FOREVER GANGSTA
GLOCKS ON SATIN SHEETS I II
**By Adrian Dulan**
TOE TAGZ I II III
**By Ah'Million**
KINGPIN DREAMS  I II
**By Paper Boi Rari**
CONFESSIONS OF A GANGSTA
**By Nicholas Lock**
I'M NOTHING WITHOUT HIS LOVE
SINS OF A THUG
**By Monet Dragun**

CAUGHT UP IN THE LIFE I II III

**By Robert Baptiste**

NEW TO THE GAME I II III

By **Malik D. Rice**

LIFE OF A SAVAGE  I II III

A GANGSTA'S QUR'AN I II

MURDA SEASON I II

GANGLAND CARTEL

By **Romell Tukes**

LOYALTY AIN'T PROMISED  I II

**By Keith Williams**

QUIET MONEY I II

THUG LIFE

By **Trai'Quan**

THE STREETS MADE ME I II

By **Larry D. Wright**

THE ULTIMATE SACRIFICE I, II, III, IV, V

KHADIFI

IF YOU CROSS ME ONCE

ANGEL I II

By **Anthony Fields**

THE LIFE OF A HOOD STAR

**By Ca$h & Rashia Wilson**

THE STREETS WILL NEVER CLOSE

**By K'ajji**

CREAM

**By Yolanda Moore**

NIGHTMARES OF A HUSTLA
**By King Dream**

## <u>BOOKS BY LDP'S CEO, CA$H</u>

<u>TRUST IN NO MAN</u>

<u>TRUST IN NO MAN 2</u>

<u>TRUST IN NO MAN 3</u>

<u>BONDED BY BLOOD</u>

<u>SHORTY GOT A THUG</u>

<u>THUGS CRY</u>

<u>THUGS CRY 2</u>

<u>THUGS CRY 3</u>

<u>TRUST NO BITCH</u>

<u>TRUST NO BITCH 2</u>

<u>TRUST NO BITCH 3</u>

<u>TIL MY CASKET DROPS</u>

<u>RESTRAINING ORDER</u>

<u>RESTRAINING ORDER 2</u>

<u>IN LOVE WITH A CONVICT</u>

<u>LIFE OF A HOOD STAR</u>

WITHDRAWN

RAWN

9 781952 936609